SEE YOU IN THE COSMOS

SEE YOU IN THE COSMOS

JACK CHENG

DIAL BOOKS FOR YOUNG READERS

DIAL BOOKS FOR YOUNG READERS

Penguin Young Readers Group * An imprint of Penguin Random House LLC

375 Hudson Street, New York, NY 10014

Printed in the United States of America

ISBN 9780399186370

1 3 5 7 9 10 8 6 4 2

Design by Jason Henry * Text set in Neutraface Slab

To Mom, Dad, and Charlie

NEW RECORDING 1
6M 19S

Who are you?

What do you look like?

Do you have one head or two?

More?

Do you have light brown skin like I do or smooth gray skin like a dolphin or spiky green skin like a cactus?

Do you live in a house?

I live in a house. My name is Alex Petroski and my house is in Rockview, Colorado, United States of America, planet Earth. I am eleven years and eight months old and the United States is two hundred forty-two years old and Earth is 4.5 billion years old. I'm not sure how old my house is.

Maybe you live on an ice planet, so instead of houses you have igloos and your hands are icepicks and your feet are snowshoes and you're covered in gold-brown fur like Carl Sagan. That's my dog. I named him after my hero, Dr. Carl Sagan, who was one of the greatest astronomers of our time. Dr. Sagan helped send Voyagers 1 and 2 into deep space and put a Golden Record on them with all kinds of sounds from our planet, like whales singing and people saying hello in fifty-five languages, and the laugh of a newborn baby and the brainwaves of a woman in love and mankind's greatest music like Bach and Beethoven and Chuck Berry. Maybe you've heard it?

I found my pup Carl Sagan in the parking lot at Safeway, and when I saw him he was dirty and hungry and hiding behind a dumpster. I said, Come here boy, don't be scared, but he was crying and curling his tail because we were still strangers at that point. I told him I'm not going to hurt him, I'm a pacifist, and I guess he believed me because when I picked him up he didn't even fight me or try to run. Then I took him back to my house and my mom was lying on the sofa watching her shows like she usually does, and I told her I got the groceries but I got a pup also and I'll take good care of him I promise, I'll play with him and feed him and give him a bath and all the stuff you're supposed to say.

And she said, You're in the way! So I got out of the way. My best friend Benji's mom would freak if he brought home a pup, but my mom, she doesn't care as long as I make us dinner and don't bother her when she's watching her shows. She's a pretty cool mom.

I don't know what kind of shows you guys have but the ones my mom likes are game shows and judge shows and shows with five ladies sitting in a fake living room. When I'm at Benji's house we watch Cartoon Network because his family has On Demand, and Benji loves *Battlemorph Academy* and so do a lot of the kids at school. I think that show's OK but I prefer the more classic cartoons like *Dexter's Laboratory* to be honest. That Dexter is one smart kid. I hate it when his sister Didi goes in and messes up everything. I'm glad I don't have a sister to mess up my stuff, especially when I'm working on my rocket.

I do have an older brother though. His name is Ronnie but everyone calls him RJ except my mom and me and some of his old high school friends because his middle name is James. Ronnie's a lot older, he's more than twice how old I am. He's twenty-four. He lives in Los Angeles and his job is an agent, and I know what you're thinking but he's not that kind of agent. He's not a spy or Bond, James Bond kind of agent. He doesn't fight terrorists or bust drug dealers or play poker with super-villains. He helps basketball and football players get shoe commercials. But he does go to fancy parties and wear sunglasses, so I guess it's kind of the same.

Ronnie wouldn't let me keep Carl Sagan at first. He never likes it when my mom and me spend his money on stuff that isn't groceries or bills for our house. When I told him about Carl Sagan over the phone he said, Uh-uh, we can't afford a dog. I said I think we CAN afford a dog because I've been getting the on-sale food from Safeway and making my own sandwiches for school instead of buying hot lunch, and also I got a part-time job helping Mr. Bashir stack magazines at his gas station. I said, I've been saving the money for my rocket but I can use some of it to buy Carl Sagan's food because he's not that big of a dog, and besides, you should come back to Rockview sometime and meet him in person—I mean, in dog—before you make any brash decisions.

That was almost a year ago and Ronnie still hasn't met Carl Sagan in dog yet. But I'm sure when they finally do meet that Ronnie's going to love him because who can turn down that face?

Huh? Who can turn down that face?

That's right, I'm talking about you, Carl Sagan. Do you want to say hello?

Come on boy, say hello.

Carl Sagan doesn't want to say hello. He's just staring at me like, What are you doing? Who are you talking to? Is there a person in there? I don't see a person in there.

There's no person in here boy, it's just an iPod. You

watched me spray-paint it gold, remember? I'm making recordings so when intelligent beings millions of light-years away find it one day they'll know what Earth was like, do you understand?

He doesn't understand. Now he's looking out the window. He's easily distracted.

So then I . . . um . . . What was I talking about?

Anyway, I thought that maybe you guys already got my hero's Golden Record but maybe you don't have record players where you are, or you used to but not anymore. The only ones I've ever seen are the used ones at Goodwill and nobody buys them because iPods and iPhones fit in your pocket better. Also, this iPod can hold a lot more than a record. I already uploaded everything from the Golden Record onto here and there was so much room left, and then I found out you can make recordings too, so I thought maybe I could record some sounds from Earth that you haven't already heard. Plus I'll explain everything that's happening behind the scenes while I get ready for my launch. It'll be like Blu-ray bonus features!

There's SO much I want to tell you guys. But it'll have to wait because Carl Sagan's sitting by the door because he wants to go pee and poop. And I still have to pack everything for my trip! I'll tell you about SHARF and my rocket next time.

NEW RECORDING 2
6M 41S

Hi again, guys! I promised I'd tell you more about SHARF and I'm a man of my word. SHARF is a rocket festival that's happening in the desert near Albuquerque, New Mexico. I'm launching my rocket there in three days!

The official name is the Southwest High-Altitude Rocket Festival but everyone on Rocketforum.org just calls it SHARF. It's an acronym. Acronyms are words made using the first letter of other words, like how NASA is National Aeronautics and Space Administration. In fourth grade we made acronyms from our own names and I used my full first name even though Mrs. Thompson said I could just use Alex. I wanted to challenge myself. The acronym for my name was:

Astronomer

Launches rockets

Earthling

Xplorer

Afraid of spiders

Nice person

Dedicated

Enthusiastic

Rocket enthusiast

I made one for my hero too. It was:

Cosmic

All-time hero

Really smart

Likes science

Everyone on Rocketforum is really REALLY excited about SHARF. There's a post at the top that says OFFICIAL SHARF THREAD and it has SO many replies already. Frances19 said she's dyeing her hair a special color for SHARF and Ganymede and Europa were talking about how much fun last year's was, and Calexico posted a bunch of cool tips about camping, like if you leave your shoes outside your tent at night make sure you turn them upside down in the morning because there might be scorpions. He said they show up in pairs too, so if you find one scorpion you'll usually find another. They're very romantic creatures.

I already packed my rocket and toothbrush and Ronnie's old tent, and a 2-in-1 shampoo/conditioner because it'll save me some room. I packed Carl Sagan's special kibble also—they're going to have barbecue food at SHARF but Carl Sagan can't eat it because he has a sensitive digestive system.

I still have more to pack but I needed a break, so I came up to the roof of my house. I love lying down on the hood of a car like Dr. Arroway in the movie *Contact* but my mom doesn't drive anymore, so I just come up on our ladder to the roof. I usually come up here at night so that way I'm closer to the stars, even though it's only one story closer.

I like coming up here during the day too though. Our subdivision is on a hill, and when I'm up here I can see really far. I can see the train tracks and Burger King and I can see Mr. Bashir's gas station which has a flagpole outside with the biggest American flag in Rockview, it's SO huge. Way in the distance I can see Mount Sam and the big white letter *R* for Rockview on the side near the bottom. One time before Ronnie's homecoming game against our town's rivals, Belmar, some kids from Belmar High came in the middle of the night and changed the

R to a *B*, and the next day Ronnie was so mad that he ran for five touchdowns and our team kicked their team's butts. I guess their plan backfired.

Sometimes after my mom has one of her quiet days she'll need fresh air so she'll go for a walk, and when I'm up here I can see where she walks. Like right now she's walking toward Justin Mendoza's house, which is down our street toward the bottom of the hill, and when she gets to Justin's house she'll either turn left toward Mill Road or turn right toward Benji's subdivision. I can't see that as good because it's surrounded by trees.

Justin's the one who gave me this iPod, actually! He was a grade lower than Ronnie in high school and he used to come over and play with Ronnie all the time, but he didn't move away after college like Ronnie did. I went over there yesterday to buy the iPod from him for twenty dollars like we agreed, but then he said I could just have it for free because the battery sucks. He went inside his house to get it and I waited in his garage, and I was looking at the Honda motorcycle he's always working on and I squeezed one of the handles, but when I did a screw fell out, so I put it on a blue rag with a bunch of other parts.

Justin came back with the iPod and charger and I said, Hey Justin, your job is a mechanic, shouldn't you be done working on your motorcycle already? He said his problem is he'll think he's done but then he'll ride around on it for a while and think of something better to do, so he'll take it apart and start over again. I told him he should just download a simulator for his motorcycle like the one I found for my rocket called OpenRocket. It lets me put in different motors and change the nose cone and fins and everything, and it tells me exactly how high the rocket's going to go so that way I don't even have to buy any parts until I'm ready to launch. I told him that's how I designed Voyager 3, my rocket that's going to carry his iPod into space.

Justin said, So it's going to be your first launch ever? And I said that's right, and he said, Shouldn't you do some test launches? And I said, That's the whole point of the simulator, it's so I don't have to, DUH!

Justin laughed and he asked me how's Ronnie doing, and I told him Ronnie's busy like usual with his prospective clients. A prospective client is someone who Ronnie wants to want Ronnie to be their agent, so he takes them out to lunch and he pays for their lunch. Justin said he really looks up to Ronnie, he's always thought of him like an older brother, and I said that's funny because I've always thought of him like an older brother too, and Justin laughed again. He told me to let him know how my launch goes and I said I will, and I told him he might want to check the handle on his motorcycle to make sure there aren't any parts missing.

NEW RECORDING 3
6M 16S

What do you guys do when you can't fall asleep?

Maybe you don't need sleep at all, maybe you're just awake all the time because your planet spins so slowly that you're always facing the sun. It's always day.

Or maybe you guys do the opposite, you pretty much sleep whenever you're not eating, like koalas or Carl Sagan. He just curls into a doughnut on the bed or sofa or my lap and he starts falling asleep, easy.

Are you sleeping right now?

I guess not, because how would you be listening to this if you were sleeping?

I guess that means we're both awake . . .

I finished packing last night. And today I spent the whole day making food for my mom for when I'm gone. My mom knows how to cook and she's a great cook, but

I've been making food for us so much this year that I'd feel bad if I didn't do something.

Plus she was having another one of her quiet days where she stays in bed and stares at all the little bumps on the ceiling. I think she likes counting them. And I brought water to her room and I told her, I made you food for the next three days when I'm at SHARF, all you have to do is take out the GladWare from the refrigerator and heat it up in the microwave and I love you.

I thought I'd be really tired after making all that food but I wasn't. I tried listening to Beethoven and Chuck Berry and watching my Blu-ray of *Contact*, but they only made me more awake. I tried sleeping in Ronnie's bed too. I keep everything on his side of our room exactly how it was when he moved out, so that way when he comes home to visit he'll see all his sexy lady posters on the wall and his sports trophies on the shelf and he'll feel like he never left. Sometimes I sleep in his bed though, because maybe if you sleep where another person sleeps and do what that person does, then eventually you'll start turning into that person. You'll think like they think and remember what they remember, and after a while you'll have big muscles and make a lot of money to buy groceries for your mom.

My Amtrak train to Albuquerque, New Mexico, leaves

pretty early tomorrow. Calexico and some other Rocket-forum members are meeting at Blake's Lottaburger which is a restaurant near the train station in Albuquerque, and they're going to carpool to the SHARF site and I'm going to get a ride. I hope I can figure out who's who because for most people I only know their usernames and not what they look like.

Also, I only have two days until my launch, so I'll have to find some real important sounds from Earth for you guys really fast. Maybe . . . maybe since you can already hear the heartbeats and brainwaves of a woman in love on the Golden Record, I can record the sounds of a MAN in love on this Golden iPod!

I would record myself but I'm not in love with anyone yet. I don't love any of the girls at school because they're mostly just excited about buying clothes and Snapchatting and Skyler Beltran. We have different interests. I'm not worried though, I bet I'll meet someone at SHARF who's in love because I know a lot of guys like that. Ronnie's in love with his girlfriend Lauren, for example, and Benji's in love with Ms. Shannon, who teaches advanced math. He said she leaned over to help him with a math problem once and she smelled like peach Jolly Ranchers. He made me promise not to tell a soul on Earth, so I think it's OK if I tell you guys.

Too bad Benji couldn't come to SHARF . . .

He's on vacation in Chicago with his mom and sister and his mom's new boyfriend.

One time Benji asked me do I feel bad about not having a dad and I asked him, Do you feel bad about not having a dinosaur? Benji said he's not sure because he's never had one, and I said I feel the same way about a dad. Benji said it'd be so cool to have a triceratops though, you could ride around on it and crash through the walls at our school and if a hall monitor tries to write you up for being late you can say, Take it up with my triceratops. I told him it was a great idea.

Sometimes I do think it'd be cool to have a dad. In *Contact*, Dr. Arroway's dad died when she was a kid also, but at least she was older than I was. She could remember looking through the telescope with him on their porch and using their old radio to talk to people in Florida. But my dad died when I was three, so everything I remember is what other people told me. My mom told me that on the day I was born my dad was supposed to be home from a work trip but he missed his flight, so she had to drive to the hospital all by herself because Ronnie wasn't old enough to drive yet. But then my dad finally got there and ten minutes later I got there.

It's almost like my dad's a jigsaw puzzle, and my mom has some of the pieces and Ronnie has some of the pieces, but a bunch of other pieces are missing so I can't finish the puzzle. This year in Mrs. Campos's social studies class we learned about genealogy, which is the study of who you come from, and we had a lab day where we went on computers in the library to a site called Ancestry.com. When you put in your name and your parents' and grandparents' names on Ancestry.com, it builds a family tree for you automatically using government records and old newspaper articles and things like that. It said that my lolo and lola and my mom's side of the family are from the Philippines, which I already knew, and it said that my dad's side of the family came from Europe on a ship in 1870. Ancestry also sends me an e-mail whenever they find out something new about my family—it's like having my own CSI, which is an acronym for Crime Scene Investigator. Except instead of solving crimes it's solving stuff about my dad, it's my DSI—Dad Scene Investigator.

Aye yai yai, I'm never falling asleep at this rate . . .

I'm going to try going to bed again. Carl Sagan and I have a big day tomorrow.

Good night guys.

NEW RECORDING 4
[RECORDING NOT AVAILABLE]

NEW RECORDING 5
8M 52S

OK, let me try this again. I wanted to tell you what happened at the train station before but I was crying and I wasn't making sense, so I deleted it.

Ronnie used to tell me to man up whenever he saw me cry. He'd tell me to stop crying, nobody likes a crybaby, and I try but I can't help it sometimes. Sometimes the clouds inside my head get big and gray and swirly and then I hurricane through my eyes. Except I don't literally hurricane through my eyes—I don't actually have a weather system in my head.

This morning just when Carl Sagan and I were about to leave, I realized that I packed too much stuff, even with my 2-in-1 shampoo/conditioner. I tried carrying it all and it was SO heavy, I could barely even make it five steps before I got tired. It didn't look that heavy last night and everything by itself wasn't heavy, but it really adds up. I said to Carl Sagan, What do we do now? and he looked at me like, Why are you asking me? And then I tried putting my duffel bag on his back and he squirmed away and he was like, What do you think I am, a donkey?

I told him I know he's not a donkey, but then I had a great idea.

My idea was to go in our garage and get the wagon that I use for buying groceries, and I put everything in the wagon and it fit, problem solved! Then I knocked softly on my mom's door to see if she was awake yet but she wasn't, so I went up to her bed and I whispered in her ear, We're leaving now, we'll be back on Sunday like I said and I love you, just in case she could hear me in her dreams.

Carl Sagan and I walked down our street and we turned left at Justin Mendoza's house. We walked along Mill Road, and I was pulling my wagon with one hand and I had Carl Sagan's leash in my other hand, and we went past Mr. Bashir's gas station and the Super 8 Motel right next to it. I wanted to say hello and good-bye to Mr. Bashir but I didn't want to be late, and also I was worried that the Amtrak people might not let me bring my wagon on the train. But I wasn't crying yet, that didn't happen until later.

We got to the Amtrak station fifteen minutes before the train was supposed to get there. I showed the ticket guy my e-ticket and he asked me where are my parents, and I said it's just me and Carl Sagan. He asked me where's Carl Sagan and I moved to the right because Carl Sagan was hiding behind my legs. The ticket guy looked at me and he said, This is an adult ticket, and I said, Yeah, because the website only let me buy an adult ticket. He said that I need a children's ticket and I asked him how can I get one, and he said I need to buy it with an adult ticket and I was really confused. He said I can't get on the train by myself, I need to have an adult with me if I'm younger than thirteen. Then he asked to see my ID and I showed him my Planetary Society membership card, and he said he needs an ID with my birthday on it so I showed him my school ID, and that's how he found out I'm not thirteen yet.

I told him I'm more responsible than a lot of thirteen-year-olds I know. I said I'm more responsible than even a lot of fourteen-year-olds. But he said it doesn't matter, the only thing that matters is your real age, and I said that's really stupid because kids are different. They should give everyone a test to see how responsible they are and then give them a responsibility age. I know I'd be at least thirteen then because I can already cook and take care of a dog.

I didn't say anything about the responsibility test to the ticket guy, though. I just thought about how I had all of my stuff and Carl Sagan's stuff and Carl Sagan too, and I really didn't want to miss SHARF, so I sat down on one of the chairs in the station and I started crying.

Carl Sagan started crying too because he cries whenever I cry, and then I thought maybe it's better if I don't go to SHARF. Maybe it's better if I just stay in Rockview because I've never been away from home without my mom or Ronnie before, and if I stay here that means I'll have more time to make recordings for you guys, and then when I have enough sounds from Earth I can launch Voyager 3 on my own, I don't have to do it at SHARF, even though I spent all that money on my train ticket and on registration and now I won't get to meet Europa or Calexico or anyone else from Rocketforum.

And that's when I got out my Golden iPod and tried telling you guys what happened, but it just came out as a bunch of crying. And I heard the horn from the train coming and I cried even harder, I didn't think I was ever going to stop.

But then I heard someone say, What's the matter? and I looked up and it was this older kid and he was wearing a blue bandanna on his head and he had a backpack that was even bigger than I was. It was SO huge.

The older kid sat down next to me and it took me a while to tell him everything. I had to stop hurricaning before I made any sense. I calmed down finally to just scattered showers, and I told him I'm supposed to go to SHARF to launch my Golden iPod into space and all my friends from Rocketforum.org are going to be there, and I spent a fortune on the train ticket and I made food for my mom and put the GladWare in the refrigerator and now there's no way I can go because I'm not thirteen even though I'm at least thirteen in responsibility years.

He said, This sounds like it's really important to you, and I said, Of course it's important, if it wasn't important I wouldn't be crying, DUH! Except I didn't say that last part, I just nodded. I'm complicated.

He asked to see my ticket and I showed it to him, and I showed him my duffel bag with my rocket and my registration e-mail and my Google Maps printout of the SHARF site and even my 2-in-1 shampoo/conditioner, I don't know why I showed him that. He asked me where are my parents and I told him my dad died when I was really little and my mom's at home, and she doesn't really care what I do as long as I don't bother her too much. He said, Man, you're starting this early, aren't you? and I said, Huh? Starting what early? And then he gave me back my folder and he told me that no matter what, just follow his lead and nod along to whatever he says, and I nodded.

He got in line so I got in line too, and when we got up to the ticket guy, the ticket guy looked at him and he looked at me and he asked the older kid, Is he with you? And the kid said, Yeah, he's my stepbrother. He said, I leave to go to the bathroom for one minute and Alex tries to ditch me at the station, some brother, huh? The ticket guy looked at me and asked me, Is he your brother? I looked at the kid and then back at the ticket guy and I nodded, and the ticket guy said, Next time stay with your brother, OK? and I nodded again. Then he scanned our tickets and he gave us our seat numbers.

The older kid helped me carry my wagon onto the train, and there's an upstairs level and a downstairs level and our seats were upstairs. We had to walk through a bunch of the train cars to get to the pet-friendly car, and between the cars they have these metal doors with big rectangular buttons on them that when you push the button the door slides open automatically and it goes *kuu-chhhhhh* like on a spaceship. It's SO cool, I wish I had those for my house!

There weren't as many people on the train as I thought, though. Probably half of the seats were empty. And I guess it was still pretty early in the morning because I saw old people and families with little kids and most of them were sleeping, except this bald guy who was wearing gray robes like a martial arts master. When we passed his seat he smiled at me and I bowed and I said Namaste, which is how you're supposed to greet martial arts masters.

I'm here in the pet-friendly car now, and Carl Sagan's curled into a doughnut on the seat next to mine. The older kid isn't here with us anymore though, he moved because he's kind of allergic to cats. I said, Shouldn't you sit in the seat number that the ticket guy gave you? And he said that they usually don't care. He said if anyone asks me am I by myself or gives me any trouble just come and find him, and I said, Thank you for pretending to be my adult. He said, No problem, I hope you find what you're looking for, and I told him I'm not looking for anything, I'm launching a rocket, remember? And the kid laughed and said, That's right, and then he left and—

Oh, DUH. I bet he was talking about the sounds from Earth I want to record for you guys. That's what he hopes I . . . Hey! Maybe the older kid has a girlfriend! And he can be my man in love! I'm going to go find him later and ask him.

NEW RECORDING 6
7M 36S

We're almost in New Mexico! Our train's definitely going full speed now too—full speed ahead!

It felt kind of weird when we started moving. The train brakes went *tsssssssss* and then the buildings next to the train station started going by, slowly at first and then faster and faster, and I thought about how with every second that passes I'm moving farther away from my house and my mom, and it's almost like Voyagers 1 and 2, how with every second they're moving farther out into space and away from THEIR home, away from the earth. But I guess the difference is that I'm coming back after—

UNIDENTIFIED CHILD: What are you doing?

ALEX: Oh, hi. I'm making recordings to send to outer space.

UNIDENTIFIED CHILD: Your dog is funny!

ALEX: He's—oh, he's just hiding under the seat because

he gets nervous around strangers. His name's Carl Sagan. I named him after my hero Dr. Carl—

UNIDENTIFIED CHILD: Did you and Car Saban see the sightseer car?

ALEX: Is that a part of the train?

UNIDENTIFIED CHILD: It's the back part of the train! It's before the lunch car and it's hecka hecka cool, it's all made of glass!

ALEX: Um, wouldn't it break if it was all glass?

UNIDENTIFIED CHILD: It's strong glass.

ALEX: Oh cool. I haven't seen it yet but I was just about to go look ar—

UNIDENTIFIED CHILD: Do you wanna play Battlemorph cards?

UNIDENTIFIED FEMALE: Lacey, honey, stop bothering that boy.

ALEX: It's OK ma'am, she's not bothering me.

ALEX: Sure, I'll play Battlemorphs.

LACEY: What's your name?

ALEX: My name is Alex.

LACEY: My name is Lacey and I'm five and a half years old. How old are you?

ALEX: I'm eleven. Is that your mom?

LACEY: Uh-huh. And that's my sister. Her name is Evan.

ALEX: That's a really weird name for a girl.

LACEY: Her name is Evan and she's three years old. Where's your mom?

ALEX: She's at home in Rockview. She's probably eating one of the lunches I made for her right now, unless she's—

LACEY: Did she make you wear old person clothes?

ALEX: You mean my brown jacket? My hero had one just like it. He had a red turtleneck like this too that he wore all the time on his TV show *Cosmos*, the original one, not the one with Neil deGrasse Tyson.

LACEY: Aren't you hot though?

ALEX: Kind of, but on Rocketforum.org they said to wear layers because it might get cold in the desert at night. I'm going to SHARF which is an acronym for Southwest High—

LACEY: One of my teachers at my school wears jackets like that. He's hecka hecka nice. He gives you three pieces of candy every time you tell on someone doing something bad, but if you get something wrong he says, Thaaaat's OK. He's hecka hecka nice.

ALEX: He sounds nice.

LACEY: Have you played Battlemorphs before?

ALEX: Yup. I played it at my best friend Benji's house.

LACEY: OK! I'm going to give you a card, and me a card, and you a card . . .

ALEX: I really wanted Benji to come with me but him

and his family are in Chicago with his mom's new boy-friend. His parents are divorced.

LACEY: Divorce?

ALEX: Uh-huh. I found out because fifth grade in gym class Benji started crying in the middle of volleyball, and Mr. Sanford asked Benji, Are you crying? and Benji shook his head to say that he wasn't but I could tell he was be-cause I was standing right next to him. Then Benji had to go to the bathroom—

LACEY: And you a card, and me a card, and me a card . . .

ALEX: —and I went to the bathroom too to see if he was OK and that's when he told me his parents were get-ting divorced. Benji said his dad said he's moving out of their house because he loves Benji and his mom, and I said, That makes no sense, if you really love someone why would you move away from them!

LACEY: My mom really loves me.

ALEX: Can I look at my cards now?

LACEY: You can look at your cards now. I dealt so I go first. I play a cocoon . . . and it morphs!

ALEX: I think you're supposed to wait—

LACEY: I play another cocoon! And it morphs!

ALEX: Um—

LACEY: It's your turn.

ALEX: OK. I'll draw a card.

ALEX: You should see Benji's collection. Benji loves Battlemorphs. He has the Trainer Playset and the Battle Enhancer app and that's all he wants to do especially when it's hot outside, he just wants to stay inside all day long and play Battlemorphs or Call of Duty.

LACEY: This one girl on my block, her name is Maya and she just wants to stay inside all day long and she's hecka hecka mean to everybody! She only likes cats—

LACEY'S MOTHER: Lacey, when we don't have anything nice to say about a person, then we . . .

LACEY: ——

LACEY'S MOTHER: We what, Lacey?

LACEY: Don't say it.

[train horn blaring]

LACEY'S MOTHER: That's right, we don't say it.

LACEY (to Alex): One time Maya told the teacher on me and my friend who's also her friend. She told him we stealed her pencil but we didn't! It was a lie. Maya's a huge liar.

LACEY'S MOTHER: Lacey, what did I just say?

LACEY: But she IS, Mama! She's a huge—

LACEY'S MOTHER: Does someone need a time-out?

LACEY: No Mama . . .

[train horn blaring]

ALEX: Hey, we're slowing down.

LACEY: We are? Why are we slowing down?

ALEX: That's weird, I don't see a town here. It's all desert.

LACEY: Mama, why are we slowing down?

LACEY'S MOTHER: I don't know, honey. Come here, come finish your fries.

LACEY (to Alex): I have to go now.

ALEX: Here are your cards back.

LACEY: It was nice playing with you.

ALEX: It was nice playing with you too.

[train horn blaring]

LACEY (distant): *Mama, can I have some water? Can I have . . .*

[brakes hissing]

ALEX: Um, we're completely stopped now. People are looking out the window trying to figure out what's going on.

ALEX: I don't think we hit anything . . . we would've felt it.

ALEX: It's hard . . . to see . . . the front . . .

ALEX: I'm going to get a better look. Hold on!

NEW RECORDING 7
6M 3S

We're still stopped. And it's been—aye yai yai, it's been almost two hours already! I think I'm getting ants in my pants, except I don't REALLY have ants in my pants. It's just an expression.

After our train stopped, one of the workers opened the doors and he said we could all get off the train if we want, we're going to be here for a while, so I took Carl Sagan out to pee and poop. And that's when I saw the ambulance.

We started walking over to see what happened, and a few other people who got off the train went over to look too. The paramedics in the back of the ambulance were talking to whoever was sick or maybe dying, and Carl Sagan and I got closer and the person was wearing an oxygen mask on his face and he was nodding and shaking his head at whatever the paramedics were asking him, and then we got even closer and I saw his face more clearly, and I saw his blue bandanna—it was the older kid!

I got a weird feeling in my stomach when I saw that it was him. It was almost like when I eat too much ice cream and my stomach hurts, I get stomach freeze, and then I don't feel like eating anything for the rest of the day. It was like that. And I think Carl Sagan had a weird feeling or maybe stomach freeze also because he was crying and hiding behind my legs even more than usual.

There was a train worker by the ambulance and I asked, What happened? Did he have a heart attack? But the train worker told me to give them some room and go back to my parents. I looked at the older kid and he looked really tired, and he looked at me but then he looked back down, I don't think he recognized me. I wanted to tell him that I figured out what he meant when he said he hopes I find what I'm looking for, but then I realized I didn't even know his name because I forgot to ask him earlier. And then the train worker told me to move back again.

So I walked backwards to give them more room but I was still watching the older kid and I wasn't paying attention, and I rammed right into someone! I said, Oops! Sorry! And I turned around and it was the martial arts master, except he was a lot shorter than I thought because before when I saw him he was sitting down. His name's Zed but I didn't know that yet, I just said Namaste again, and he reached in his robe and he took out a chalk-board that was the size of an iPad, it was his chalkpad, and he wrote on it, Your Brother? and he pointed at the ambulance.

I looked at the older kid again and then I looked back at Zed, and he didn't seem like the kind of person who would give me any trouble because martial arts masters only fight if they have no other choice. So I told him No, that's not my brother. He erased his chalkpad and wrote on it, Traveling Alone? And I said I'm not, I'm traveling with Carl Sagan, and then we both looked down at Carl Sagan who was hiding behind my legs.

Zed crouched down and I thought he was going to do some crouching-tiger kick but he was just saying hello to Carl Sagan, and Carl Sagan went up and sniffed Zed's hand and then he went back behind my legs. I asked Zed, Why do you use a chalkpad to talk, did you lose your voice? and he wrote on it, Vow Of Silence. I asked him what's his name and he wrote on it, Zed.

We watched the ambulance paramedics take the older kid's blood pressure and shine a small flashlight into his eyes, they were giving him a checkup like my doctor in Rockview, Dr. Turner, gives me every year. After that they took off the kid's oxygen mask, and Zed wrote on his chalkpad, Good Sign, but then they put the kid's backpack in the ambulance too, so I wasn't sure if it was a good sign after all. Then the train worker told us he should be fine but they're taking him to the hospital anyway, just in case.

Even though the ambulance drove away already and we're all back on the train now, we still haven't moved yet. I don't know what's taking so long . . . Shouldn't we be—

What is it, Zed?

[chalkpad sounds]

Zed just wrote, Is Everything OK?

Sorry Zed, I just—I have ants in my pants because Carl Sagan and I are going to SHARF in New Mexico to launch my Golden iPod into space. We're supposed to carpool with people from Rocketforum.org and they're going to be waiting at Blake's Lottaburger near the train station, but I don't know if they'll still be there when we get there.

[chalkpad sounds]

You too? Wait, YOU'RE going to SHARF? I thought you were a martial arts master!

[Zed laughing]

What's your name on Rocketforum? And where's your rocket!

[chalkpad sounds]

Zed just wrote, Don't Use Internet. And underneath it he wrote, Friends' Rocket.

Then does that mean you don't have a cellphone either?

Zed just nodded.

But what if we get there really late and your friend and the other carpoolers think we're not coming and they leave without us because nobody called them?

[chalkpad sounds]

Zed says we'll figure out a way.

I don't know, Zed. I really hope so . . .

I still don't get why we're not moving yet though . . .

[chalkpad sounds]

Oh, no, I HAVEN'T seen the sightseer car. But this girl Lacey said it was all made of glass so maybe we should go look. Maybe we can see why we're not moving! Great idea, Zed!

[Zed laughing]

NEW RECORDING 8
5M 27S

We're FINALLY moving again. We were stopped for so long! Me and Zed are here in the sightseer car now except it isn't all glass like Lacey said, it's more like half glass, but the windows really ARE huge though. They curve up all the way to the ceiling and there are chairs that face the windows, so you can watch the scenery go by like you're watching TV.

Once the train started moving finally everything outside went from flat desert to hilly desert, and Zed watched the scenery and I was watching Zed, and his eyeballs would move back and forth really quick when he looked at the rocks and brown bushes going by. Zed kind of reminds me of my science teacher Mr. Fogerty who's really fat and has gray hair, except Zed's not as old and he's a little smaller and he has no hair. He's like a bald Hobbit version of Mr. Fogerty—

[loud laughter]

That's Zed laughing again. I only just met him and he already laughs more than anyone I know. And when he laughs his whole body gets smaller and then bigger like blowing up a balloon.

[Zed laughing]

It's happening again!

I told Zed I still can't believe he doesn't use the internet. I said, How can you not have internet! and I told him I don't know what I'd do without internet because then I definitely couldn't learn new stuff as fast. I couldn't go on Rocketforum or YouTube and I never would've found out about SHARF or how to build a rocket, and I couldn't have Ancestry.com be my Dad Scene Investigator. Zed wrote on his chalkpad, Tell Me More, so I told him that one of the things that Ancestry.com found for my dad was a license to practice civil engineering, and I googled what's a civil engineer and it said it's someone who designs roads and bridges and things like that.

Zed held up his chalkpad again and it still said Tell Me More, so I told him that after I found out, I called Ronnie and asked him, Hey Ronnie, did you know our dad was a civil engineer? And Ronnie said, Forget about Dad, it doesn't do any good to dig up the past, and I told Ronnie I can't really forget because I have nothing to remember in the first place! And then the whole time Zed's chalkpad

still said Tell Me More, so I told him about Benji and Carl
Sagan and my mom and my school and I kept telling him
more and more, I told him SO much about everything.
Zed's a great listener, I guess because he doesn't talk.

[Zed laughing]

What's so funny, Zed?

Hey Zed, why did you make a vow of silence in the
first place?

[chalkpad sounds]

Really? How much did you talk if you talked too much?

[chalkpad sounds]

I don't know if I'd like not talking. Can we try it?

[chalkpad sounds]

[chalkpad sounds]

[Alex laughing]

[chalkpad sounds]

[Zed laughing]

[chalkpad sounds]

[both laughing]

Hey Zed, I have a question—are you in love with anyone? I'm trying to record the sounds of a man in love on
my Golden iPod.

Zed? Did you hear me?

[train clattering]

[Zed laughing]

Zed just shrugged his shoulders again.

You mean you don't know? How can you not know? Isn't it easy to tell when you're in love with someone? Do you have a wife, or girlfriend?

[chalkpad sounds]

Zed just wrote Ex-wife. I guess that means you're not in love anymore, Zed.

[Zed laughing]

Hey Zed, you know you're breaking your vow of silence when you laugh like that. Maybe you should do a vow of not talking instead, that would be more accurate.

[Zed laughing]

I wonder, do you guys have vow of silences where you are?

Do you guys even talk?

Maybe you communicate with pheromones like ants, or you make symbols in the air like sign language.

Maybe you have ten senses instead of five and you use one of the other senses to talk but you don't call it talking, you call it something else, or you don't call it at all, you something else it.

Or maybe your whole language is laughing and you have laughs that mean you're happy and laughs that mean you're hungry or that you haven't seen your brother in a long time and you miss him. How do you laugh the words, I'm so excited for SHARF? Ha ha HA hee HA? Ha HA hee ho ho HA ha?

[Zed laughing]

NEW RECORDING 9
7M 4S

We weren't two hours late to Albuquerque. We were two and a HALF hours late. When we finally got there the sun was already starting to set and the sky was light yellow, and there were a lot of people and cars. Zed helped me carry down my wagon from the train and I said let's hurry up and go to Blake's Lottaburger, but then Zed's friend was already waiting at the train station!

His name is Steve in real life and SteveO on Rocketforum, and I found out he's roommates with Zed and they live in LA, which is an acronym for Los Angeles. I said, Hey Zed, why didn't you tell me Steve was going to be waiting at the station and why didn't you tell me you live in LA? and Zed just shrugged like, You didn't ask! And then I asked him and Steve do they know my brother Ronnie because Ronnie lives in LA too and he's an agent and everyone calls him RJ. Steve said they don't know him.

Steve is a little older than Ronnie but not as old as Zed. He's more regular height too, and he has light brown hair and a goatee except it's not that thick yet so it's just a *kid*tee—

[Zed laughing]

UNIDENTIFIED MALE: Come on, I just started growing it!

ALEX: That's why I said it's a *kid*tee, Steve! It's not all the way grown yet.

[Zed laughing]

STEVE: Yeah, whatever.

ALEX: Anyway, when Steve saw Zed, he said it's about time, he can't believe the train got delayed for so long, and when he saw me he said, Wait, you're the one carpooling with us? And I said, I am?

ALEX: What happened was that everyone else at Blake's Lottaburger went ahead but Calexico told Steve I was on the train too, and since he was waiting for Zed anyway, Steve said he could drive me. He didn't know I was a kid though, and I told him I'm eleven but at least thirteen in responsibility years, and he asked me where are my parents and I told him my mom's at home and my dad died when I was really little. And then Steve looked at Zed and Zed shrugged like he was saying, Some people just grow up without dads. Even though Zed doesn't talk, I think I'm starting to understand him.

STEVE: I didn't know you were going to have a dog with you either and—hey, can you make sure he doesn't slobber all over the window back there?

ALEX: OK. Come here, boy! Come sit down next to me again. You can look at the desert later.

[dog collar tinkling]

STEVE: Thanks. And careful with the seat too. My girlfriend's going to be mad if the seat's all dirty. She's always nagging at me about how I need to get my car washed and the inside vacuumed.

ALEX: It sounds like cleanliness is really important to her.

[Zed laughing]

STEVE: Yeah, I suppose . . .

ALEX: I guess that's why you wanted us to finish our fries before we got in the car, huh Steve?

ALEX: Steve got us some fries from Blake's Lottaburger before he came to the station.

STEVE: Yeah. I would've gotten you a burger too but I wasn't sure if you were vegan like Zed. See, Zed? This is exactly why I'm always telling you that you should get a cellphone again.

ALEX: But how is Zed supposed to talk on the phone if he has a vow of silence?

STEVE: He can send texts at least.

ALEX: Hey Steve, what was that thing wrapped in

bubble wrap in your trunk? Was that your guys's rocket? It looked huge!

STEVE: Yeah, I'll show it to you after we—

[phone ringing]

STEVE: Hang on.

[headset beeping]

STEVE: Hi honey, what's up?

STEVE: Sorry, I was going to call—

STEVE: I know that's what I said. Zed's train was late, and we're also giving a ride to this kid who—

STEVE: I said I'm sorry.

ALEX (whispering): *Hey Zed, who's Steve talking to?*

STEVE: It's just the weekend, yeah. We'll be back Monday afternoon, we're stopping in—

[chalkpad sounds]

STEVE: I'm not, it's just I already said we'd be gone for the weekend.

STEVE: Two weeks ago.

STEVE: What is it?

STEVE: Look, I'm sorry. But I did tell you—

ALEX: *His girlfriend sounds mean.*

[Zed laughing]

STEVE: That was nothing. Just Zed.

STEVE: Look, can we talk about this when I'm back? I'm sorry I wasn't—

STEVE: OK. Bye.

[headset beeping]

[car passing]

ALEX: That was Steve talking to his girlfriend. He has a headset, which is a thing you put in your ear that lets you drive and talk at—

STEVE: Hey Alan, can you—

ALEX: My name's Alex.

STEVE: Sorry—Alex. Can you not do that right now? I just want to listen to music.

ALEX: OK.

NEW RECORDING 10
9M 46S

It was halfway dark when we got to the SHARF site.
And now it's all the way dark, and if my voice sounds quiet
to you guys, it's because I'm whispering. I think most
people are asleep.

We haven't had time to meet anyone yet. Calexico and
the other carpoolers were already in their tents and RVs,
which is an acronym for Recreational Vehicles. The site
here is just really flat desert with wide mountains in the
distance, and when I first saw the tents and RVs on our
way in, it felt like we were driving toward a colony on
Mars, except instead of being red and orange it was gold
and brown and a little purple.

I really should've practiced setting up my tent before
I came. Steve parked his car in front of where our tents
were going to go and he kept on his headlights so we
could see, and I was watching him and Zed set up their

tent and trying to do what they were doing. But it's harder than it looks. Also, Carl Sagan kept standing on our tent and I know he was just trying to help but it wasn't making things any easier, so I started yelling at him to get off and he started crying.

I didn't mean to get mad at him, I was just frustrated because the guys had their tent set up already and ours was still two-dimensional.

I guess Zed heard my yelling or Carl Sagan's crying because he came over, and I held on to Carl Sagan's leash while Zed set up my tent. He almost had to stand on his tippy-toes to reach over to hook the middle hooks onto the wobbly poles, but he got it finally and then my tent wasn't two-dimensional anymore. It could stand by itself. I put Carl Sagan inside and then we staked everything to the ground with the tent stakes, which look like upside-down letter *L*'s, they don't look anything like stakes you use to kill vampires.

Steve turned off his car lights and put on his head-lamp, which is a flashlight you wear on your forehead and it shines wherever your head's looking. It's SO cool. We moved all our stuff into our tents and then Zed pointed at him and Steve's tent like, Do you want to come hang out?

I told him thanks for the invitation but maybe later because I have to finish gluing my rocket. I said I brought my rocket in sections because otherwise it wouldn't fit in my duffel bag, so I still have to glue the sections before the launch tomorrow because the glue needs time to dry.

Zed stood there for a second and then he gave me a thumbs-up, and then he went into him and Steve's tent and I went in mine and glued my rocket. I had to hold my flashlight with my feet while I glued the sections, I wish I had two extra arms or at least a headlamp, and it took me FOREVER to glue everything. Except not really forever because that would mean I'm still gluing them. It took like an hour. By the time I finished, Carl Sagan was already asleep, and I looked outside at the guys's tent and it was still glowing.

I went over and I said, Are you guys still awake? and Zed unzipped the tent door and let me in, and him and Steve's tent was even bigger than it looked from the outside, it was SO huge. Except not as huge as the Quidditch World Cup tent in Harry Potter because that's just a movie and it's special effects. The guys's tent could probably hold like seven people.

I sat down on Zed's sleeping bag because Zed had a round pillow he was sitting on, and Steve was sitting on his own sleeping bag. His headlamp was hanging from a clip in the ceiling like a chandelier and he was holding a small can of something, and I said, Hey Steve, are you drinking Red Bull?

Steve took a sip and told me it's like Red Bull but way

better. He said it's an energy drink called LOX, which is an acronym kind of for Liquid Oxygen, and he showed me the can and it said *Human Rocket Fuel* under the logo. Steve said there's not really liquid oxygen in it though, but there ARE vitamins, so it gives you a lift and it's healthy for you too and rocket fuel is just a metaphor for how it makes you feel. I asked him what's a metaphor and he said a metaphor is when you describe something using something else because otherwise it'd take too long to explain.

Steve asked me do I want to buy some LOX, he's selling them at SHARF for two dollars each, and also if he can get three people who get three people to sell LOX, he gets a free BMW, and if I get three of my friends to get three of their friends to sell LOX, then I can get a free BMW too. I told Steve no thanks, I can't drive a car yet and also I'm saving my money for food and emergencies, but Ronnie might want a BMW because he's an agent so I'll ask him the next time I call him.

Steve said he still can't believe my mom and Ronnie let me come here by myself, and I told him they usually don't care what I do as long as I don't bother them too much. Then Steve and Zed looked at each other, and then Steve said he wishes his parents gave him that kind of freedom when he was a kid. I told the guys about Ronnie's job and then I found out that Zed was on my same train because he was in Colorado for a retreat. I asked Zed, What were you retreating from, was it an army of ninja warriors? And Zed laughed and shrugged again like he doesn't know, but then Steve said it's a different kind of retreat—it's when a group of people go away somewhere for a few days to think. I told the guys I'm thinking all the time, I don't have to go anywhere specific to do it.

Oh, I finally saw the guys's rocket, by the way! Steve brought it in from his car and it was white and blue and as tall as I am almost, and it was SO cool. Steve named it Linda after his girlfriend. He's entering it in the contest for the Civet Prize, which is a $50,000 prize for the person or team who can send a rocket 200,000 feet into the air and then recover it intact. Steve said they're going to win for sure because him and Zed's other roommate Nathan designed their rocket, and Nathan's a genius at math, but he couldn't come this weekend because he had to work overtime at his computer programming job.

Steve said he's really excited for tomorrow because $50,000 is no joke, and I said, That reminds me, do you guys know any astronomy jokes? Because I'm always looking for good astronomy jokes. They said they don't, so I told them one that I know.

I said, Why do moon rocks taste better than earth rocks?

Because they're a little meteor.

At first nobody laughed, and I thought maybe they didn't understand the joke so I explained that it's funny because moon rocks are little meteors, but meteor also sounds like *meatier*, like, the word that means something has more meat on it, and meat tastes good, even though realistically moon rocks probably wouldn't taste that good because they don't really have meat on them, get it?

And Zed started laughing finally, and I said, Whew, good thing I explained it, and then he laughed even louder! Steve laughed too, then he said the joke out loud, not the whole joke but just the punchline. He said, So wait, moon rocks taste better because they're a little meteor, and then he laughed again.

After we all had a good laugh Steve got another call from his girlfriend and he was trying to talk to her quietly at first but then he was talking louder and louder, so he went to his car so he could talk with her as loud as he wants. And then I thought that maybe Steve can be my man in love because he has a girlfriend, and I told Zed about it and I thought I saw him frown but maybe it was just dark, because then he laughed and shrugged his shoulders again.

Steve came back right away, I guess he didn't feel like talking with his girlfriend for that long, and as soon as he got back he unzipped his sleeping bag and started fluffing up his pillow. He said it's getting late, he really needs to go to sleep because he's exhausted from driving by himself and waiting for the train, and I said, Hey Steve, maybe your LOX doesn't work so good if you're already tired! Zed laughed and then he wrote on his chalkpad, Let's Look At Stars. I thought it was a great idea.

I unzipped the tent door and Zed and I went outside, and we looked up and I could see SO many stars, even more than in Rockview. I heard Zed write something so I shined my flashlight at him, and his chalkpad said, Crystal Clear. I said I don't think it is really, because Benji has some crystals and they're kind of cloudy, and the sky tonight's a lot clearer than a crystal. I told Zed it's more like glass right after you wipe it with Windex.

Zed wrote on his chalkpad, Tell Me More, and I told him that my parents met on a night just like this, my mom told me the story when I was eight. She said she was in college and she was working part-time at the bank, and my dad went in to cash a check. When they saw each other, it was love at first sight. He asked her can he take her out to dinner, and she said no at first but he was charming and he convinced her, and after dinner they went to the top of Mount Sam on the tramway and when they got up there they looked out over all of Rockview and up at the stars and that's when they had their first kiss. I told Zed it was probably like in Contact when Dr. Arroway meets Palmer Joss and they sit under the stars in Arecibo and have THEIR first kiss. It was probably just like that.

Then I told Zed I wonder what my mom had for dinner. I wonder which of the GladWares she reheated, was it the one with carrot and potato soup? Or maybe the Spam and rice and scrambled eggs because she felt like having breakfast for dinner. And Zed was really quiet but he's always really quiet, but for some reason he seemed even quieter than normal. After a while I heard the wind blowing but it wasn't a sandstorm, it was just a light breeze, and I looked around at the tents and RVs and some of them still had their lights on.

I told Zed, Isn't it interesting how every tent and RV has people in it, people like us with rockets they want to launch, and tomorrow we're going to meet them and see their rockets and show them ours?

And I shined my flashlight at Zed because I thought he was going to write something on his chalkpad but he didn't, he just kept looking up at the sky.

NEW RECORDING 11
6M 23S

Hi guys! There weren't any scorpions in my shoes this morning unfortunately. If there were I would've recorded their sounds for you guys, although I'm not even sure what they sound like. I think they hiss like snakes?

Maybe desert scorpions only show up if they know you're asleep, and I didn't sleep at all last night. I tried to but the ground was really hard even though I had a sleeping bag, and the glue smell from my rocket was giving me a headache. I could hear snoring coming from the guys's tent too, I'm pretty sure it was Zed. He'd snore and snore and then stop and it'd be quiet, and I'd think he was done but then he'd snore a really loud one, like FIVE TIMES as loud. It was SO loud. Maybe Zed laughs and snores extra loud to make up for all the sound he can't make during the day because he doesn't talk.

I'm kind of glad I didn't sleep though, because I got to

see the sunrise when I came out of my tent. The faraway mountains were pink and yellow, and I started brushing my teeth with the water from my water bottle, and then there were two small dots in the distance that got closer and closer and the cloud of dust behind them was getting bigger and bigger. Then they came into the SHARF site and it was a van and a truck with a trailer in the back, and that's when I remembered—TODAY IS LAUNCH DAY!

I can't believe it's already here. The people from the van and truck started setting up tents that weren't like mine or the guys's tents, theirs were just roofs but no walls. And then they took out folding tables and chairs from the trailer and tied up a big banner that said SOUTHWEST HIGH-ALTITUDE ROCKET FESTIVAL and a smaller banner that said REGISTRATION, and I said, HOLY bleep! and my toothbrush fell out of my mouth.

I rinsed off the dirt and then I grabbed Voyager 3 from my tent, the glue was dry by then, and I ran over there to register and that's when I recognized one of the organizers—it was Ken Russell from K&H Rocketry Supply!

I recognized him because he posts YouTube videos on Rocketforum that he records from his store in New Mexico, and he has a bushy red beard and he was wearing a green polo shirt just like in his videos. He was taking out a bunch of power cables from the trailer and I said,

Hey Ken, I love your videos and I ordered all the parts for my rocket from you, do you remember sending a big package to Alex Petroski in Rockview, Colorado?

Ken turned around and he looked surprised to see me but then he smiled, and I remembered that he has a huge gap in between his front teeth. I bet he's really good at whistling. Ken said he does remember my order, actually, and then he saw Voyager 3 in my hands and he said, Is that it? And I said, It is, and he told me it's a nice-looking rocket. I told him I want to register but I have a question because I'm not sure which contest to enter, because I'd love to compete for the Civet Prize except my rocket's carrying my Golden iPod into space, so it isn't coming back down to Earth.

Ken looked at my rocket again and he was quiet for a little while, and then he asked me what kind of motor am I using. I said I'm using a D-class motor but the Open-Rocket simulation told me it's going to go high enough to leave the atmosphere. Ken said, Is that so? And I said, It is, and he said I should just enter it in the D-category contest because that's the one for D-class motors, but hold on a minute because he has to finish getting stuff out of the trailer.

I asked Ken where are the launches happening and he pointed to a clear part of the desert away from the tents, and then he started getting the launchpads from his trailer.

When I saw them I said, THOSE are the launchpads? They don't look like launchpads at all! They had launch rods but instead of pads they were big wooden things that looked like Olympic track-and-field hurdles—they were launchurdles.

Ken carried out the launchurdles and I helped him plug in all the cable wires, and then we sat down at one of the tables and he found my name on his laptop in the list of people who registered online. Ken typed the letter *D* for D-class in the column next to my name and he said I'm ready to go, I'm the first official entrant! And then he asked me am I here by myself and I said I came with Steve and Zed and Carl Sagan but they're all still asleep.

I asked Ken can I borrow his laptop to check my messages because Benji told me he'd send me some pictures from Chicago, and Ken said Sure, knock yourself out, and I said I'm not going to do that because I'm a pacifist and besides, how am I going to check my e-mail if I'm unconscious? And Ken laughed and I wondered if food ever gets stuck in the gap between his teeth.

I logged into my e-mail but there wasn't a message from Benji like I thought. The only e-mail I had was from Ancestry.com and it said, We found possible matches in the Petroski family tree.

I logged into Ancestry and under where it said U.S. Public Records, I saw my dad's name, Joseph David

Petroski. I clicked on it and saw his name again on a document called the Nevada Marriage Index, and it's so weird, it said there's someone who has the same exact name and birthday as my dad except in Las Vegas instead of Rockview. It said he's married to some person named Donna but that's not my mom's name, and besides, my parents got married in Colorado, not Nevada, so I'm pretty sure it's just a coincidence. That happens sometimes—Ancestry.com will send me stuff about people with the same name as my dad but who aren't really my dad, even though this is the first time it's someone with the same birthday too.

Anyway, I just closed my e-mail and I told Ken thanks for letting me use his computer, and now I'm back here by mine and the guys's tents. Carl Sagan's awake and Steve went to get breakfast for all of us, and Zed's sitting on his round pillow away from the tents and staring in front of him, I think he's meditating.

Some of the other campers are waking up too, and more people are starting to get here in their cars and—Oh! I think I recognize that person. I think that's Frances19! Oh wow, her rocket's bright purple and so is her hair!

Come on, Carl Sagan! Come on, boy!

[dog collar tinkling]

Let's go make some friends!

NEW RECORDING 12
5M 17S

Every. One. Is. So. AWESOME.

I've never met so many people who love rockets and space as much as I do. There are some kids here like me but mostly grown-ups and I'm the only kid who didn't come with their mom or dad. A lot of people were surprised I came here by myself but some of them said, Seeing from your forum posts, I'm not surprised at all. I showed them Voyager 3 and my Golden iPod and my Planetary Society membership card and they all said, Wow, that is so cool. And I thought Carl Sagan was going to be nervous around so many people and cry and curl his tail and he did at first but then he loved everyone and they loved him. They all said it was a great name for a dog.

Oh! I finally met Calexico! I thought he was going to be Ronnie's age but he was a lot older than that even, he had long white hair in a ponytail and he was wearing

a tie-dye shirt that said *Peace Love and Rockets*. A lot
of people here have really cool shirts that I want. Fran-
ces19 has a shirt that says *Angular Momentum: It Makes
the World Go Round*. Ganymede and Europa both have
shirts that say *Save Pluto* and they both have earrings too
except on their lips—they have lip rings. I also met Dish-
gal and Bebop and BuzzAldrin who isn't the real Buzz
Aldrin, he just picked that name because Buzz Aldrin is
his all-time hero, and maybe also because he has short
hair like a buzz cut. BuzzAldrin told me he lives in Las
Vegas and I said there's someone in Las Vegas who has
the same name and birthday as my dad, isn't that weird?
And he said yeah, that's really weird.

I already saw so many people's rockets too! Most
of them are huge and shiny and, um, way bigger than
Voyager 3. But the coolest rockets were definitely the
college teams's. They're all here trying to win the Civet
Prize and their rockets are SO huge, they're even bigger than Steve's rocket! One of the teams's rockets is
called Skywalker II and it's named after Luke Skywalker
from Star Wars. Another of the teams's rockets is called
Ptolemy IV and it's named after Claudius Ptolemy from
Ancient Greece. The teams all have their own launchpads and trailers too, and they all have sponsorships
from big companies like CivSpace and MST Engineering
and Praxa Aero.

A lot of people said they hope Lander Civet is going to be here but they also said they don't have their hopes up. They just have their hopes in the middle. Lander's the CEO of CivSpace and he's the one who started the Civet Prize, but he's probably really busy right now because his company is launching their Mars satellite next week. I always see articles on Rocketforum and in Mr. Bashir's magazines about how Lander wants to start a human colony on Mars. One time I saw him on the news and he's bald like Zed and he wears suits all the time like Ronnie, and the news reporter asked him why is he spending his entire fortune trying to go to Mars, couldn't he use it for something else?

People used to ask my hero stuff like that too. They'd say, We have so many problems here on Earth, we have global warming and wars in the Middle East and kids in Africa who don't have food or clean water, so why should we try to go to Mars or communicate with extra-terrestrial intelligence when we can't even solve all the problems we have on our own planet?

And do you know what my hero said to those people? He told them to think about what it would mean if we went to Mars. He said if we can do something that big, something that's never been done before in the history of humanity, then of course we can solve all the problems we have at home, DUH! And I agree.

And even though Lander Civet's not at SHARF, some people from his company are. On Rocketforum you can tell who's from there because it says CivSpace in front of their names, and here you can tell because they're all wearing gray polo shirts with the CivSpace logo on the pocket. I talked to CivSpaceElisa and CivSpaceNelson who are on the Jupiter team, and CivSpaceScott who's on the PR team, and PR isn't a planet like Jupiter, it's an acronym that means Public Relations. I told Scott that if they ever discover a new planet they should call it Public Relations so that way his team can have a planet too. Scott laughed and then he gave me some stickers.

Elisa told me she loved the OpenRocket screenshots I posted when I was designing Voyager 3 and my cheeks started getting warm, it's a really hot day today. She gave me her business card also and she said if I'm ever looking for a summer internship, they'd be glad to have me. I asked her what's an internship and she said it's a job where you get paid in knowledge. I told Elisa that the internship sounds really interesting but I'd like to keep my options open because Mr. Bashir already pays me five dollars a week to help him stack magazines at his gas station. I told her he lets me take home the science magazines he doesn't sell every month, so with my job right now I get paid in knowledge but I get paid in money too. Elisa said that I'm a tough negotiator. She said we should keep in touch and talk about it with my mom before the next school year ends, and she wished me good luck with my launch.

My launch! I can't believe it. I'm launching my Golden iPod into space!

NEW RECORDING 13
5M 28S

CROWD: Three . . . two . . . one . . .

[high-pitched roar]

[clapping and cheering]

ALEX: HOLY bleep. That one went so high!

ANNOUNCER: *All righty folks, that about wraps it up for our C-class launches. Let's give our contestants one more round of applause.*

[clapping and cheering]

ALEX: OK guys, this is it, my last recording. I can't believe it's only been a day since I left Rockview on the Amtrak train!

ALEX: Voyager 3 is already set up on the launchurdles next to all the other rockets, and Carl Sagan and I are standing by the registration tents next to all our new friends. After lunch even more people showed up, and even before the contests started some people were launching their rockets just for fun, and there were more dogs and NASA shirts and dogs with NASA shirts and Calexico was playing guitar and singing songs I didn't know and—

ANNOUNCER: *Next up, we have the D-class. That's D as in Discovery, D as in Danger, which also happens to be my middle name.*

[polite laughter]

ANNOUNCER: *Just trying to lighten things up here, folks.*

[dog barking]

ANNOUNCER: *OK! First up in the D-class, we have Joel and Noah Turner from Santa Fe, New Mexico. Step on up, guys! Let's give 'em room everybody . . .*

ALEX: I know I didn't get to record as much for you guys as I wanted, I was too excited meeting everyone and seeing their rockets and T-shirts and lip rings and purple hair that I forgot to record more! But I guess I did get the sound of trains moving and the sound of cars on the highway, and the desert at night and Steve talking on the phone with his girlfriend who he's in love with probably and—

ANNOUNCER: *This is Joel and Noah's second SHARF festival, last year they took first place in the egg loft . . .*

ALEX: —and now you know what the launches at a rocket festival sound like! Isn't it SO exciting? Maybe after my launch I can get another iPod and build another rocket, I can build Voyager 4, and then next year I can come back to SHARF and launch that too, and then I'll do Voyager 5 the year after and—

ANNOUNCER: *All righty folks, it looks like they're ready to go. Let's count it down for them!*

ANNOUNCER: *Five . . . four . . .*

ALEX: Three . . . two . . .

CROWD: One . . .

[high-pitched roar]

[clapping and cheering]

ALEX: It's still going!

[popping sound]

ALEX: They have two parachutes!

ALEX: That was a good one too.

ANNOUNCER: *A mighty fine start for the D-class. I have a feeling that's going to be tough to beat. While Noah and his dad go retrieve their rocket, let's get ready for our next contestant, Alex Petroski!*

ALEX: IT'S MY TURN! Guys this is it!

ANNOUNCER: *Alex is here all the way from Rockview, Colorado. You might've seen him around today, looking like a spittin' image of the late, great Dr. Carl Sagan. Alex, come on up!*

ALEX: I'm coming!

[hurried footsteps]

ANNOUNCER: *Where are you going, Alex? The controls are here under the tent.*

ALEX: I have to put something in the payload!

ANNOUNCER: *Looks like we have some last-minute adjustments, folks.*

ALEX: OK guys, I hope you like all the recordings I made. I'm putting in the charger cable with the Golden iPod so that way you can charge it, and I wish I had something beautiful and poetic to say like my hero would about how we're all hurtling through the vastness of space on a mote of dust suspended in a sunbeam and stuff like that but I don't, so I guess, um, just let me know if you get these recordings! Bye! I mean, hello!

[rustling]

[muffled clapping]

ALEX (distant): *OK, I'm ready!*

ANNOUNCER: *He's ready, folks. Let's give him a countdown! Five . . . four . . .*

CROWD: *Three . . . two . . . one!*

[high-pitched roar]

[rattling]

[crowd oohing]

[clipped thud]

NEW RECORDING 14
7M 47S

[wind blowing]

[fabric fluttering]

. . . can't believe . . . [muffled] . . . still works . . .

I thought it was broken for sure.

[sniffling]

You guys are probably thinking . . . You're thinking, how can he still be making recordings if Voyager 3 is in space?

Voyager 3 didn't make it into space. It didn't even go a hundred feet before . . . be . . .

[sniffling]

I'm not making any sense again.

I shouldn't have yelled at that kid Noah afterwards. I didn't mean to say that stuff about his dad doing all the work for him. I don't hate that kid, I just felt bad because my rocket failed and his went really high, and my rocket

didn't even go half as high as his did. That rocket simulator didn't work at all . . .

I did apologize to Noah, though. He accepted my
apology, and his dad said it's OK, it's no big deal. Everyone told me it's OK, they've all had rockets crash and
there's always next time. I said I know there's next time
but it's my fault that there wasn't this time.

I let my excitement get the better of me, and it left the
worse of me behind, and the worse of me did a bad job
of gluing Voyager 3 in the dark.

[sniffling]

On the Golden Record there isn't anything about the
times our rockets failed, even though they did. That's because my hero wanted to put our best foot forward. He
didn't want to put in anything about our rockets exploding because what if you guys saw that and thought we
were trying to make them explode on your planet? Then
you'd probably be scared and hide from us. Or maybe
you'd try to blow us up before we could do it to you.

But my hero also said that knowledge is better than
ignorance, and it's better to find out and embrace the
truth even if that truth might not feel good. I wanted to
put my best foot forward just like my hero, but I believe
in the truth too, so that's why I'm telling you guys what
happened . . . why I'm telling you my rocket crashed.

The worst part is that I was so close. I was here at

SHARF and it was a beautiful day and I made so many new friends and they were all watching, and I could've prevented the crash if only I was more careful. Or if only I practiced launching my rocket ahead of time.

I thought this Golden iPod got destroyed too, I thought I lost all my recordings and now I had nothing left, and I went back to my tent and I was crying and so was Carl Sagan, and I hugged him really tight and stuck my nose in his fur and we cried together.

And then, I don't know, I kept thinking about that Ancestry.com notification, the one that said there's somebody with the same name and birthday as my dad but in Las Vegas, and I'm still thinking about it even now, and I keep thinking, what if that person in Las Vegas actually IS my dad? I know my mom and Ronnie said my dad died when I was three, but what if he's still alive and they just don't know he's still alive. Like, what if when he had his accident instead of dying he got amnesia, and when he woke up he forgot everything except his name and birthday and he didn't know he had a family in Rockview. What if that's what really happened? Then shouldn't I go to Las Vegas to see if it's the truth, to find out if it's really him? My hero believed in the truth, after all, and so do I.

I wasn't thinking most of this until just now though. I was still hurricaning before and my tears were making Carl Sagan's fur wet, and it was even worse than at the train station, it was probably a Category 4 or 5 hurricane. Then I saw a shadow on my tent and I unzipped the door and it was Zed, and he was holding his chalkpad but it was blank and I told him to go away. I was mad at Zed too, I don't know why.

CivSpaceScott and Elisa came up to the tent then also, and they were carrying some of the pieces from Voyager 3, and I tried to tell them I'm sorry my rocket failed and if they don't want to give me an internship anymore I understand.

But they gave me the rocket pieces and Scott told me it's OK, it happens to the best of us, in fact, it happened to CivSpace when they were launching their Cloud 1 rocket. And I said, It did? and Scott said yes. He told me they were still a very young company then and they spent so much time working on Cloud 1, and everyone was working nights and weekends for eight months straight leading up to the launch.

But when the launch finally happened, there was a malfunction with one of the fuel lines and the rocket exploded. Scott said after it happened everyone felt so bad, and some people were crying just like I was crying, because they felt like they did all that work for nothing.

He asked me do I know what happened then? and I shook my head, and he said Lander Civet went up in front of the whole company and made a speech. Lander told everybody that they knew from the beginning there were going to be failures, this IS rocket science after all, and that this was only their second try. He said that right now was the most important moment—how they reacted to the failure. They could either let it stop them or they could redouble their efforts, figure out what went wrong, and fix their mistakes so they can make the next try a success. Lander Civet told them that there was no way he was going to give up, and he hoped they wouldn't either.

Their next rocket only took them three months to build instead of eight, and it's the same rocket that carried their Zeus spacecraft to the International Space Station. I wasn't crying as much after Scott told me that.

Elisa gave me my Golden iPod then, and she said, Look, it still works, and I pushed the middle button and the screen lit up like normal. Elisa said the Civet Prize launches are starting soon, do I want to watch it with her and Scott? And I thought about what Lander said about learning from their failures, and I told Elisa I do want to watch, but first I want to make a recording for you guys. I said I have to keep making these recordings because I want to redouble my efforts, just like Lander said.

And now I'll go watch the Civet Prize launches and learn from the college teams about how they build their rockets, and then I'm going to build Voyager 4, and if that fails too then I'm going to learn from those failures and redouble my efforts again, I'm going to quadruple my efforts to build Voyager 5, and I'll go to Las Vegas and I'll find my maybe dad and if he's my real dad and he got amnesia then I'll help him remember he has a family, because then he can help me build my new rockets just like that kid Noah's dad helped him, we can build them even better and faster, and then my dad can be my man in love because he's in love with my mom and we'll all come back to SHARF next year as a family, Ronnie too, and we'll launch our rocket with the Golden iPod into space together and it'll be so great. No—it'll be better than great. It'll be perfect.

NEW RECORDING 15
7M 58S

Hi guys, a lot of people left already.

Only a few of us are still here. The launchurdles are gone and the registration tents are gone, Ken Russell took those down after the awards ceremony, and in the morning we'll all be gone too. So if someone drives by tomorrow and looks out the window of their car, all they'll see is flat desert. They won't even know anything was here, because they looked too late.

Maybe after you get my Golden iPod you'll come to Earth and by then there won't be humans on our planet anymore, because you looked too late. And all you'll have are these recordings to tell you what happened. I guess that's why it's important that I keep making them—so when you come here, you'll know what it was like.

The rest of the launches yesterday were so good, guys.

I learned SO much from watching them. And even though Steve's rocket went really high it didn't go as high as the college teams's. Steve was so mad afterwards. He was even madder than I was! He called his roommate Nathan on the phone and started yelling at him, and when Skywalker team went to recover their rocket, Steve said he hopes that it crash-landed and they don't win the Civet Prize. Then during the awards ceremony, Steve was saying how him and Nathan's rocket could have done a lot better if they had big sponsors too, and they should put a camera on THEIR next rocket like Skywalker team did so they can post the video on YouTube and make some ad revenue. I think Steve was jealous.

That kid Noah and his dad ended up winning the D-class contest, by the way. I watched them go up for their gold trophy and K&H gift certificate and I tried to remember what Lander said about redoubling my efforts. But I was happy for Noah and his dad too—they built a really great rocket. And then afterwards at the barbecue Ken Russell came up to me and he gave me a K&H shirt!

I said, What's this for? And he said it's a special prize for Best First Effort, and I tried on the shirt and it was SO big, the only size he had left was adult XL which is an acronym for Extra Large. I said, You don't have anything smaller? and Ken laughed and he said, You'll grow into it, and his bushy beard was fluttering in the wind a little bit. It's a very majestic beard.

Ken gave me his business card also, and he said if I'm ever in Taos, New Mexico, to stop by the store and say hello. I asked him is Taos close to Las Vegas? and he said Las Vegas is a lot farther west, and I borrowed his laptop again to figure out how much farther, and then I was trying to change my Amtrak ticket to go to Las Vegas instead of back—

Oh look, Zed's coming with the wood! One of the college teams was taking apart their launchpad and Zed went to see if they'd give us the wood for a campfire. Steve's going to be really happy now because he kept talking about the fire earlier, after he stopped being mad. It was all Steve could talk about besides talking about his LOX and his girlfriend.

[wood clattering]

Hey Zed, our fire's going to be huge with all THAT!

[Zed laughing]

I think Zed's going to start the fire now. He's putting some dried sticks and bushes in a pile on the ground and—

What? Oh, sure, you can use some of it.

[paper tearing]

Zed wanted a couple blank sheets of paper from my notebook.

Now he's crumpling them up and putting them with the dried bushes. I think he's going to rub two sticks together until they start smoking and—

Oh, no wait, he has a lighter.

Hey Zed, isn't that cheating?

[Zed laughing]

The paper's on fire now. Some of the dried bushes are too.

Now Zed's adding the smaller pieces of wood.

Hey Zed, Steve was right, you really are a pro at this!

[Zed laughing]

Anyway, what I was saying was that I went on Ken's laptop and I tried to change my train ticket to Las Vegas, but it said that to change it I have to pay an extra fee of—

Sorry, Zed—what?

[chalkpad sounds]

That's what I said, Las Vegas.

[chalkpad sounds]

Because my maybe dad lives there.

[chalkpad sounds]

I thought he died too, but then Ancestry.com said there's someone in Las Vegas with the same name and birthday as him, so I thought maybe he didn't die, maybe he got amnesia instead, and—

[chalkpad sounds]

You don't have a phone or laptop! How can I show—

[chalkpad sounds]

Oh yeah! We can get Steve. But what about the fire?

[chalkpad sounds]

Oh OK. Let's go get him, then.

Hold on, guys. I have to show Zed something.

NEW RECORDING 16
7M 16S

Hi guys, I'm back.

We found Steve after my last recording and he was trying to sell the rest of his LOX to the people who were still here. When Steve saw us he said, How's the fire going? And I looked back by our tents and the fire burned out because Zed stopped adding wood to it. I told Steve, It's not going so good but can I see your phone? I want to show Zed something.

I logged into my Ancestry.com account and I showed the guys my maybe dad's name and birthday in the Nevada Marriage Index, and I said, See guys? It's the same as my real dad's.

And Steve said, So what? It's probably just a coincidence, and I said that's what I thought too but isn't it a really WEIRD coincidence, that not only do they have the same name but the same BIRTHDAY also?

Steve asked me did my parents ever get divorced and remarried, and I said No, after my mom and dad fell in love on Mount Sam they got married and had Ronnie and thirteen years later they had me.

Zed wanted to see the phone, so I gave it to him, and he gave me his chalkpad and chalk to hold on to and he started googling stuff on the phone, he was typing so fast.

I said, Hey Zed, what happened to not using internet! And I thought he was going to laugh but he was really concentrated on the phone. And then he showed me and Steve a website that said my dad's name, and underneath it was an address in Las Vegas, Nevada.

Steve and Zed looked at each other and then Zed looked at me, and I gave him back his chalk and chalk-pad because it looked like he wanted to write something. Zed wrote, We're Already Going, and he showed it to Steve, and Steve said, We're already going?

He looked at me and then back over at Zed, and then he said, No, uh-uh, we're not taking him with us.

I said, Taking who with you? Taking me? Taking me with you where?

And Steve said, Forget it, it's not happening, it's practi-cally kidnapping, and Zed wrote on his chalkpad, Father Quest, and then Steve said, No, no more quests, I'm sick and tired of your quests! Steve was getting really mad again, I think he has anger management issues.

Zed kept waving his arms though, and Steve kept saying no way, and I said, Will somebody please tell me what's going on! And then on the chalkpad underneath where it said We're Already Going, Zed wrote, To Vegas.

I said, YOU'RE going to Vegas? LAS Vegas? That's perfect! Can I go with you?

But Steve said no, I can't, and then he turned to Zed and he said, Besides, what the bleep would we do afterwards, we can't just leave him there! And Zed wrote on his chalkpad, Ronnie.

I think he meant that Ronnie is in LA, and since the guys live in LA too, they can just take me to see Ronnie afterwards. I told him that was a GREAT idea.

Steve said no way, Las Vegas was supposed to be HIS time, and I said, Your time for what? and then Zed erased his chalkpad and he wrote on it, More Important, and Steve said, For him maybe, but not for me! and then Zed underlined More Important and waved his chalkpad again. I've never seen Zed so excited.

Steve said it's probably not my dad anyway, and even if it is, there's probably a really good reason that my mom and Ronnie aren't telling me about it, and I told Steve he's right, there would HAVE to be a good reason why, and I think the reason is my dad got amnesia and forgot he had a family in Rockview. I said, Maybe if I go to Las Vegas then I can help him remember who he is, and I can bring him back to Rockview and he can be with my mom and love her and hug her like she told me he used to do, and they can sleep in the same bed together and in the mornings I'll knock softly on the door and I'll say, Are you guys awake yet? and they'll be just starting to wake up and then I'll crawl into the bed and get in between them because it'll be a cold morning but we'll have a blanket and we can all keep each other warm, and then Carl Sagan will come and jump on the bed too and we'll all laugh because we're surprised, and we'll say, Oh Carl Sagan, what a silly pup.

I looked at Zed and he wasn't waving his chalkpad anymore. And then he looked at Steve and Steve frowned, and then he told Zed, If we bring him, YOU'RE going to have to watch him while I take care of business there.

I said, What business? And he said, It's personal. And I said, What about my Amtrak ticket though, I spent good money on that ticket, and Zed wrote on his chalkpad, Try To Get Refund, and he pointed at himself.

And then Steve said, Hold on, let's not get ahead of ourselves. He said I should call my mom first and ask her did my dad ever live in Las Vegas, and second, call Ronnie and ask him the same thing, and only if they both say it's OK for me to go, then they'll drive me.

I borrowed Steve's phone and called my mom but she didn't answer, probably because she was having another one of her quiet days. So I left her a message saying I'm at SHARF and everything's great even though Voyager 3 failed, and I made so many new friends and Ancestry.com said there's someone in Las Vegas who has the same name and birthday as Dad so maybe he's still alive and he just got amnesia, and Steve and Zed can take me to see if it's really him because they're going to Las Vegas on their way back to LA, and afterwards they'll drop me off at Ronnie's place so I might not be home for another day or two and I hope that's OK because I know I only made you food for the weekend and I love you.

Then I called Ronnie, and I could tell he was busy doing something else like reading sports news because whenever he's busy like that he'll just say Uh-huh to whatever I say. Actually it was perfect because the best time to ask for Ronnie's permission for stuff is when he's not paying attention.

I said, Hey Ronnie, I'm at SHARF right now and I got this notification from Ancestry.com, and he said Uh-huh, and I said, And I found out some stuff about our dad but I'm not sure if it's the truth or not, and he said Uh-huh, and I said, And Steve and Zed can take me to investigate because my hero believed in the truth and so do I, and he said Uh-huh, and then I was going to tell Ronnie I'm coming to LA afterwards to visit but I thought it might be funny to surprise him so I said instead, How's the weather in LA this time of year? and he said Uh-huh. And I said, Oh, it must be a pretty nice time to visit, huh? and he said Uh-huh, and then he said, Hey listen, I gotta go meet a prospective client but make sure Mom stops running the AC so much, the electric bill was really high again this month. I said OK, I'll tell her, and then he said, Talk to you later.

I know that Ronnie didn't really say yes. But he didn't say no either. And I can't wait to see his face when Carl Sagan and I show up at his doorstep in LA, maybe with our maybe dad! And I can't believe I'm going to Las Vegas! And then LA!

Can you believe it, Carl Sagan? Can you believe it, boy?

[dog collar tinkling]

Carl Sagan can't believe it either.

NEW RECORDING 17
3H 7M 15S

[soft pattering]

Do you guys hear that?

Listen.

That's the rain.

It started raining last night, and I didn't know it rained so much in the desert but it does. Zed wrote on his chalk-pad, Monsoon Season, and there were clouds in the distance that were big and fluffy at first but then they dissolved and looked like huge gray curtains, they were rain curtains, and they had bends in them from the wind just like real curtains. Here in the desert you can see the wind, even when you can't feel it.

It's still dark outside right now.

It's almost five o'clock in the morning.

I slept a little better this time, the ground didn't feel

as hard for some reason, but I still woke up after only a few hours.

And I've been looking at the picture of my family that I keep in my wallet in the pocket under where I keep my Planetary Society membership card, and I wonder, Does my dad still look like he does in that picture?

Does he still have a big smile and dark brown hair?

Maybe he grew a kidtee like Steve or a majestic beard like Ken Russell, or maybe he started losing all his hair so he decided to shave it off like Zed.

Maybe he laughs as much as Zed does. Or even MORE than Zed. And when he gets sick he gets better really fast because laughter is the best medicine.

Zed built a great fire last night, by the way. Steve kept saying that he still doesn't think it's a good idea for me to go with them to Las Vegas, but once Zed got the fire going again Steve warmed to the idea, I think because the fire warmed him. We sat around it in some camping chairs that Calexico had, he was still here at SHARF too, and he brought his guitar and he was strumming it without playing any songs. And most of the time we all just stared at the campfire because fire is really interesting to watch, I'm not sure why. Maybe it's because it's always changing.

Carl Sagan was watching the fire too, at least at first. He was lying down next to my feet and after a while I could see his back go up and down the way it does when he's asleep. And then I looked around and Calexico was asleep too, he fell asleep with his mouth open and his guitar in his lap, and Zed's eyes were closed also but he wasn't snoring so maybe he was just meditating, and Steve was drinking LOX again and eating a hamburger that was left over from the barbecue.

Then I looked up and I thought I saw a bunch of shooting stars but they weren't stars because it was cloudy, they were just the ash from the campfire, and I felt the ash hit me on the head and shoulder but it wasn't the ash, it was the rain starting. Carl Sagan woke up then and so did Calexico, and we folded up the chairs and put out the fire, and we came back in our tents . . .

[rain intensifying]

Does it rain where you are?

Is it raining right now as you're listening to this message?

That would be so weird.

Maybe it never rains where you are, but it's always cloudy because your planet is a gas planet. And you guys look like balloons with really long noses, and instead of walking you float through the clouds.

Or maybe you're like bright beams of light, and when someone looks at your planet from space it looks the way the earth looks at night with all those glowing cities, except instead of streetlights and buildings glowing, it's just your people.

Or maybe you're like mirrors, and when you stand in front of someone you see a reflection of their reflection of your reflection of their reflection, all the way to infinity.

Benji's mom has a round mirror in her bathroom that she uses for her makeup, and when I'm in there I like to point that mirror at the mirror on the wall, so that it goes to infinity.

It's still dark out . . .

It's not raining that hard but . . .
the tent makes it sound

a lot more

it's so . . .

[light snoring]

[rain intensifying]

[rain easing]

[rain stopping]

NEW RECORDING 18
11M 15S

[loud pop music]

ALEX: . . . ey . . . an . . . yo . . . [muffled]

[music fading]

STEVE: Did you say something?

ALEX: I said, Can you turn down your music? I'm making a recording.

STEVE: Oh. Sorry.

ALEX: Thanks Steve.

ALEX: Guys I have some great news! I have a new favorite restaurant. My old favorite restaurant was Burger King but we just left my new favorite restaurant a couple of hours ago and they have the best cheeseburgers on Earth and the fries are thicker than my fingers and there's apple pie à la mode which is French meaning With Ice Cream.

The restaurant is called Johnny Rockets, and I know what you're thinking but Johnny Rockets doesn't have any real rockets. I made the same mistake. I asked the guys, Why doesn't Johnny Rockets have any real rockets or even model rockets and why does everything in here look so old? and Zed wrote on his chalkpad, It's Nostalgic. Nostalgic is something people really don't need anymore but still like to have around, like jukeboxes or roller skates or appendixes. Do you guys have appendixes?

I'm sorry I couldn't record anything until now. I fell asleep during my last recording and the battery died. This morning when we left SHARF I asked Steve can I charge my Golden iPod on his car's USB which is an acronym for, um, I'm not really sure what, but I had to wait because Steve was already charging HIS phone because his battery died too. Probably because he was talking and texting with his girlfriend a bunch.

You guys didn't miss much though. Most of the time we were driving—we already drove through the rest of New Mexico and all of Arizona and it's already dark again! Steve really wanted to get to Las Vegas ASAP which is an acronym for As Soon As Possible, and I did too. He said we're only stopping for food and gas, so make sure I go to the bathroom when we stop, but then once we started driving he didn't drive very fast. He drove the speed limit. I said, Hey Steve, if we want to get to Las

Vegas ASAP then we should drive faster like in *Contact* when Dr. Arroway hears the signal at the Very Large Array and gets in her car and drives back to the control center and—

STEVE: I already said—I don't want to get a speeding ticket, all right?

ALEX: But Zed drove really fast when you guys switched for a while, and HE didn't get a ticket.

STEVE: Well, Zed's gotten plenty of tickets. You'd think with all that meditating he does he'd drive less like a maniac.

ALEX: Steve has a good point, Zed. You did drive like a crazy person.

[Zed laughing]

[chalkpad sounds]

ALEX: Is that an astronomy joke, Zed? Because you know how I love astronomy jokes.

STEVE: Let me see. Oh—that's one of his Zen koans.

ALEX: What's a Zen cone? Is it a joke that has a point, like the nose-cone of a rocket?

[Zed laughing]

[knocking on chalkpad]

ALEX: Zed wants me to read it out loud. It says, What's The Sound Of One Hand Clapping?

ALEX: That's easy, Zed. It's just like the sound of two hands clapping, except softer. See?

[soft patting]

[Zed laughing]

STEVE: Zed loves that kind of stuff. Did he tell you that he used to be a motivational speaker? Before he moved in with me and Nathan.

ALEX: Really?

STEVE: Yeah, his whole thing was about helping short guys like him have more confidence. He wrote a bunch of books about it too—there should be a couple back there, check on the . . .

[rustling]

[pages flipping]

ALEX: Oh wow. You guys, Zed wrote almost as many books as my hero! Except instead of being called *Pale Blue Dot* or *Cosmic Connection*, they're called *As Tall As You Think You Are* and . . . *The Extra Six Inches: How to Project Confidence, Earn Respect, and Attract the Woman of Your Dreams.*

STEVE: You know, I've been reading them and there's actually some really good stuff in there. It's a real shame you stopped doing that, Zed. Speaking and all.

ALEX: Why did you stop, Zed?

[cars passing]

STEVE: He stopped because after his divorce he had a nervous breakdown while he was onstage. And then he went to India to find some guru but he never found the guy, and when he got back he gave away most of his money to charity. I still can't believe you did that, Zed.

STEVE: I keep telling him that he should write a new book about his divorce and going to India and everything. I could help him sell it too. There's that woman who wrote a book about that kind of stuff and it was a number one bestseller!

ALEX: Steve, you're always coming up with ways to make money or BMWs. You're very entrepreneurial.

STEVE: You think so? I guess you're right. Yeah.

ALEX: Zed's just staring out the window now. Hey Zed, did you turn into Carl Sagan?

[Zed laughing]

ALEX: I know what'll cheer you up, Zed . . . an astronomy joke!

[Zed laughing]

ALEX: OK, how does an astronaut cut his hair on the moon?

[car passing]

ALEX: Zed gives up.

ALEX: The answer is . . . Eclipse it.

ALEX: It's funny because the word *eclipse* also sounds like *HE clips*, so that's how the astronaut is cutting his hair, he's clipping it, though in reality it'd be pretty hard to do that on the moon because how is he supposed to cut his hair without taking off his helmet?

[Zed laughing]

ALEX: I'm glad you like my joke, Zed! I have—

STEVE: Look, there it is!

ALEX: There what is?

STEVE: Vegas.

ALEX: Let me see—oh WOW! Look, Carl Sagan, look at the lights!

[dog collar tinkling]

ALEX: Guys, I wish you could see this right now. Las Vegas is straight ahead in front of us and with all the lights it looks like a galaxy or a nebula of orange and white stars. And the way we're going toward it and the cars around us are going toward it, it's almost like we're moths going toward a light on somebody's porch—

[chalkpad sounds]

[Alex laughing]

ALEX: Zed says they should call it Moth Vegas.

ALEX: Good one, Zed!

[Zed laughing]

ALEX: Hey Steve, can I borrow your phone so I can put in my maybe dad's address on your Google Maps?

STEVE: Um, maybe we should wait until tomorrow to see him. It's already pretty late and it's still going to take us a while to get to the main part of the city.

ALEX: Oh . . .

STEVE: Hey, don't blame me, it was Zed's idea to stop and eat at Johnny Rockets earlier.

ALEX: Also, we could have done the drive-thru and just ate in the car but you didn't want to. I would've been careful, Steve! I know your girlfriend cares about cleanliness.

[Zed laughing]

STEVE: Yeah, whatever.

ALEX: Then when we get to Las Vegas, are we just going to go to sleep?

STEVE: No way! Las Vegas is the best at night. Everything's all lit up and they have casinos and restaurants and stores and clubs that are open twenty-four hours, it's like the biggest funnest shopping mall ever.

ALEX: That does sound like fun.

ALEX: Oh! I thought of some more sounds I could record for you guys—

STEVE: For . . . what?

ALEX: I'm talking to *them*.

STEVE: Oh, sorry.

ALEX: It's OK, Steve! Anyway, I thought that since I already got some sounds of Steve talking to his girlfriend, and I'll probably get some sounds of my maybe dad, after

I help him remember he's in love with my mom, that then when we go to LA we can record Ronnie in love with his girlfriend Lauren. The more the better!

ALEX: Hmm . . . since it's the twenty-first century, I should probably also put on the Golden iPod the sounds of a man in love with another man, and a woman in love with another woman . . .

ALEX: The man and a man is easy because Nolan Jacobs has two dads, but how am I going to get a woman and a woman? I don't know anyone who's a lesbian. I think my substitute math teacher Ms. Jeffers might be a lesbian but even if she was, I'd still need to find another one for her to be in love with because only one lesbian isn't going to do me any good.

[Zed laughing]

ALEX: What's so funny, Zed?

ALEX: Hey Steve, do you guys know any lesbians?

STEVE: Um, I think I'm Facebook friends with a few.

ALEX: That's perfect! Can we record them, and also do you know where I can get a stethoscope and a brain scanner?

STEVE: I don't know them *that* well.

ALEX: Oh, OK.

ALEX: Maybe we'll meet some lesbians in Las Vegas.

NEW RECORDING 19
3M 53S

We're in the sky! We're at the top of the Stratosphere! Except it doesn't go all the way to the real stratosphere, not even close. The Stratosphere I'm talking about is a hotel and casino and space needle in Las Vegas. I asked Zed, Why do they call it a space needle if it doesn't go into space? and Zed wrote on his chalkpad, It's Nostalgic.

Las Vegas is so huge, guys. There are SO many lights everywhere. There are like a million building lights and streetlights and car lights going up and down the streets, and the lights go on for as far as I can see. There are parts with really dim lights too, I think that's where the houses are, and maybe my maybe dad is in one of those houses. It's hard to tell though, because the only buildings I can see clearly right now are the hotel and casinos. There's an Eiffel Tower one and a Caesars Palace one, and a medieval castle and New York City and a big glass pyramid and sphinx and it's like the wonders of the whole earth smushed into one place. Maybe if you guys ever come visit us you'll land in Las Vegas first, and then right away you can get a pretty good idea of all of human civilization.

They don't let pups into the Stratosphere, so Steve's watching Carl Sagan right now. I hope he's doing OK without me. After we got to Las Vegas we found a motel that allows dogs and then we parked our car, and then we walked down the Las Vegas Strip which is the main road. There were tons of palm trees and lights of all different colors and like a million people too, and Carl Sagan was getting SO nervous. He was crying and hiding behind my legs and I had to pick him up because my feet were getting tangled in his leash. I told him, It's OK boy, you're safe with me, but I could feel him shivering even though it's so hot out, Carl Sagan was so scared.

Oh! I found out what Steve's personal business is. I don't know why he didn't want to tell me about it before. When we were walking, Steve was giving out his business card to people and telling them he'll pay cash for their cellphones and just text his number. I was surprised so many people took his card—don't they need their phones for emergencies? Steve said people go to the casinos and they spend all their money but then they want to keep playing, so it kind of is an emergency, and he helps them by giving them money for their phones. Steve's very thoughtful.

Do you guys have casinos where you are? Me and Zed had to walk through the casino downstairs to come up here to the observation deck, and it was like an arcade except with even more lights and noise. It was so loud, I couldn't even hear myself think sometimes. We watched people playing the slot machines and every once in a while someone would win a bunch of money but they didn't even yell or get excited, they just kept playing like they didn't win any money at all. I'd get really excited if I won that money because then I could buy all the parts I'd ever need for Voyager 4, but they won't let kids play the casino because you have to be at least twenty-one years old which I'm not, even if you use my responsibility age.

Maybe my maybe dad wins a lot of money at the casinos . . . I wonder if he's been up here to the top of the Stratosphere. Maybe he came up here after he got amnesia, and he looked out at the Las Vegas lights and he had a funny feeling because it reminded him of being on top of Mount Sam with my mom. Except he didn't know why he had the funny feeling because of his amnesia.

Maybe when I meet him tomorrow I can ask him did he have a funny feeling on the top of the Stratosphere, and if he says yes, I can tell him why and help him remember.

I wonder if he's going to have strong arms. When he hugs me and lifts me up in the air is he going to make noises like a rocket taking off? Or is he going to think I'm too old for that kind of stuff.

Is he—

Oh. OK, Zed.

Zed says we should go, they're closing the observation deck.

NEW RECORDING 20
6M 52S

It's a lot quieter in Las Vegas when you're not on the Strip.

It's a lot darker too.

The brightest lights I see are the tall lights in this parking lot, and they have a bunch of moths flying around them. There are SO many moths, it really is Moth Vegas.

I can't wait to tell Carl Sagan about the Stratosphere. I wonder if he's tired. Steve said they call New York the city that never sleeps but Las Vegas is a city that never sleeps too, and he's right. It's 1:28 in the morning and I'm not sleepy at all, and the Zelda's parking lot is almost full so I guess there are a lot of other people who aren't sleepy either.

Zelda's is some kind of, um, weird casino. I thought it was going to be like the castle from the video game but it's not, and it's not like the huge casinos that have a hotel on top either. It's a lot smaller and the inside looked like an old basement except darker and filled with card tables and tons of people, and I had to hold my nose because the whole place smelled like an ashtray. It smelled SO bad.

Zed's already been inside for five minutes now . . .

I hope he didn't get lost. And I hope Carl Sagan's OK because he usually gets nervous around loud music like they're playing in there.

I don't know why Steve would even bring him here. Why didn't they just stay at the restaurant bar?

I think I'm starting to get ants in my pants again.

We didn't even know Steve and Carl Sagan were here until we went to the restaurant bar where Steve was doing his personal business. When we first got there we didn't see them, and I looked in the bathroom and they weren't there either, so Zed went up to the bartender and he wrote on his chalkpad, Phone? and the bartender asked him, Are you Zed? and Zed nodded like Yes.

The bartender gave us a note and it was from Steve, and it said, Went To Zelda's BRB, which is an acronym for Be Right Back. I asked Zed, What's Zelda's and when's Steve coming back, I thought we were supposed to meet him and Carl Sagan here. Zed shrugged like he didn't know, but then it looked like he was trying to figure out something in his head. Then Zed wrote on his chalkpad,

Let's Go To Zelda's, so I asked the bartender, Can you tell us where's Zelda's? and he said it's close by and he told us where.

We walked behind the restaurant bar across the parking lot and down the street and across two more parking lots here to where Zelda's is, and we went inside and it was loud and crowded and freezing cold too, they had their air-conditioning turned on SO high. And the waitresses bringing drinks to people were all wearing silver bead necklaces and headbands with feathers, and then the security guy—

UNIDENTIFIED MALE 1: Yo, yo, check that out—

UNIDENTIFIED MALE 2: Whoa! What's that kid doing here haha.

UNIDENTIFIED MALE 1: Hey kid, did you get lost?

ALEX: No mister, I'm just waiting for my friends.

UNIDENTIFIED MALE 2: He called you mister haha! *No, mister.*

UNIDENTIFIED MALE 3: What's the matter kid, they wouldn't let you in?

ALEX: Yeah, that's exactly what—

[men laughing]

[loud music]

ALEX: —happened.

[music fading]

ALEX: Um . . . Anyway, I was saying—

[loud music]

STEVE: —totally irresponsible!

[music fading]

STEVE: Why didn't you guys just wait for me!

ALEX: Um . . .

STEVE: Did you even read the note that I left you, Zed? I know you don't talk but you can READ, can't you?

ALEX: Steve?

STEVE: So what part of BRB don't you understand? *Be right back.* This is supposed to be the hottest place around here! TripAdvisor said it's where all the locals—

ALEX: Hey Steve?

STEVE: Not now, Alex. You know how long I had to wait to get in, Zed? And for a seat too! I had to stand and watch for twenty minutes—

ALEX: Where's Carl Sagan?

STEVE: —finally I got a seat and the dealer was really into me, I could tell. She kept smiling at me—

ALEX: Steve.

STEVE: —I mean I was on a winning streak! You saw how all those people were cheering me on. I could've doubled my money! I was just gonna play a few more hands and then go right back—

ALEX: But Steve—

STEVE: I said not now. Look, Zed, couldn't you just watch him for another—

ALEX: STEVE.

STEVE: What is it!

ALEX: WHERE'S CARL SAGAN?

STEVE: Where's Carl Sagan . . .

ALEX: THAT'S WHAT I SAID.

STEVE: You don't have him?

ALEX: Of course I don't have him! YOU had him at the restaurant bar and I didn't see you until now so how could I have him!

STEVE: But I tied the dog to the No Parking sign over . . . I thought . . .

ALEX: What? . . . There's nothing . . .

ALEX: He's not there . . .

ALEX: Where is he?

STEVE: Um.

ALEX: WHERE. IS. HE. WHERE IS—

NEW RECORDING 21
6M 18S

UNIDENTIFIED MALE: Here Alex, tell them what's happening.

ALEX: There's no point! How's that g . . . to . . . him . . . [muffled]

UNIDENTIFIED MALE: Sometimes it helps just to talk things out.

ALEX: I'm sorry . . .

ALEX: I'm trying to be brave.

UNIDENTIFIED MALE: You're very brave.

UNIDENTIFIED MALE: I'm going to talk to a manager. Maybe their security cameras saw where he went. We'll find him, all right?

ALEX: OK . . .

[sniffling]

[loud music]

[music fading]

Hi guys . . .

I'm sorry I got mad again.

I was mad at Steve especially . . .

[sniffling]

He was saying it's not his fault we lost Carl Sagan, and the leash must've broken or something, and I yelled at him.

I said, What do you mean it's not your fault! Why did you leave him alone, he's not supposed to be alone!

He hates being alone . . .

[sniffling]

Steve kept telling me to stop crying but I couldn't. I was hurricaning even harder than when my rocket failed. And I was so mad at Steve that I threw my Golden iPod at him.

I haven't been taking very good care of my stuff. Or my best non-human friend . . .

[sniffling]

Steve went to look for Carl Sagan in the parking lot, and the whole time he was saying, The dog has to be here somewhere, he couldn't have gone far.

And I asked Zed why does Steve keep calling him the dog, he has a name and it's Carl Sagan. And then Zed picked up my iPod from the ground and he crouched down in front of me, and he said, We'll find Carl Sagan, and I said, You talked!

I was so surprised that Zed talked.

That's him you heard just now.

I told Zed, I'm sorry I made you talk. Zed put his chalk-pad on the ground and his piece of chalk on the ground too, and I watched it roll away from the chalkpad and I started crying even harder.

Zed told me, You have to be brave if you want to find Carl Sagan, and I said, How can I be brave when I'm so sad we lost him and scared we won't be able to find him, and I'm so worried he's going to starve?

And Zed said that's exactly how, because if you're only brave when you're happy then it's not bravery.

I'm trying to be brave now . . .

[sniffling]

I wish I could call Ronnie . . .

But it's almost two a.m. and he never likes it when I call him in the middle of the night and wake him up.

Ronnie would know exactly what to do in this kind of situation. He always has a plan.

One time, when I was five, my mom took us to the big shopping mall in Belmar to get him new basketball shoes for his birthday, and Ronnie went to go get the shoes by himself and I went with my mom to a store that had all kinds of different soaps, and I was smelling some of them but then I turned around and she was gone.

I walked around the mall trying to find her and I was

crying because I thought I lost her, but then Ronnie found me and he asked me where's our mom and I said I don't know, and he said let's look for her together. So we looked for her together and then we finally found her sitting by the fountain in the middle of the mall . . .

[sniffling]

Have you ever lost someone you love?

Did you ever find him or her again?

How did you do it?

Maybe you don't have that problem because you're never separated from anyone you love.

Maybe as soon as you love someone you're physically connected to them with a tube that's kind of like a leash, except it's made out of flesh and it grows out of your belly button and you call it a fleash.

Or maybe you guys have something else, something even better, and I know my hero said that traveling backwards in time might not be possible but, I don't know, maybe you guys discovered some new law of physics that makes it possible, and one day you'll hear this recording and you'll come back in time and help me find my pup, or at least you'll send me some plans through a satellite, except instead of being for a transporter like in *Contact* they'll be for some kind of shield that I can build, like, some kind of force field that goes up and covers the whole earth and prevents bad stuff from happening, anything bad at all, like asteroids crashing or the sun getting too big, or your mom having too many quiet days or your brother moving away from home or you losing your best non-human friend outside of a weird casino.

Can you do that for me?

Please?

Can you?

Hello?

NEW RECORDING 22
2M 43S

Carl Sagan's still missing.

We looked for him all night but we didn't find him, and came back to the motel because the guys were tired, and now it's almost 4:30 in the morning.

I guess Las Vegas does sleep after all.

I'm not hurricaning or thunderstorming as much anymore. I've been trying to be brave like Zed told me. The manager of Zelda's said they don't have any security video of the spot by the No Parking sign, but then he told us that Las Vegas has a twenty-four-hour animal control hotline.

We called the number with Steve's phone and I talked to the animal control lady whose name was Cheryl, and she asked me does Carl Sagan have tags and I said yes, and she said they don't pick up animals with tags. I said, But what if his collar came loose when he ran away or someone dognapped him and put his collar on a similar dog to steal his identity? And Cheryl said, I'm sorry honey, and I said, It's not your fault, it's my fault because I never should've let him out of my sight, and then I started crying a little again.

Cheryl said she can check to see if they have him anyway, and she asked me what does Carl Sagan look like, and I told her he has gold-brown fur and floppy ears and an unusually long body. Cheryl put me on hold but when she came back she said they don't have any dogs by that description. She asked for my phone number and I gave her Steve's, and she said they'll call us if they pick up my pup.

After I called animal control we looked for Carl Sagan in the Zelda's parking lot again. We looked under all the cars and behind their tires and in the other parking lots next to Zelda's also. Then we got in Steve's car and drove around nearby but we didn't find Carl Sagan in any parking lots or by any dumpsters either, and it was probably three o'clock in the morning by then. Steve said maybe we should retrace our steps, and I thought that was a good idea, so we went back to the restaurant bar where Steve was doing his personal business earlier but Carl Sagan wasn't there. I thought maybe he picked up my scent and went to the Stratosphere after Zed and me left, so we went there but he wasn't there either. Then

I thought maybe he followed my scent from there to the restaurant bar and now we're both looking for each other and never finding each other because he's always one step behind, and maybe we both realized we're going around in circles so we both stopped to wait for the other person or dog.

I wanted to look for Carl Sagan even more but Zed said it's going to be light again in a couple of hours, let's get some rest and look for him then, he'll be easier to spot during the day. Steve said we can go to Office Depot when they open and make some MISSING DOG posters too, so now I'm just waiting for the sun to rise.

NEW RECORDING 23
7M 4S

I called animal control again this morning. It was a man this time, it wasn't Cheryl, and I gave him a description of Carl Sagan again. He put me on hold to check, and then he came back and he said they don't have him.

We already put up a bunch of MISSING DOG posters. We went to Office Depot this morning and then we went to all the places we were yesterday and put them up, we went to the restaurant bar and to Zelda's and to all the supermarkets nearby to check the dumpsters. And I kept expecting to see him, I kept expecting Carl Sagan to jump out from behind a dumpster or a truck tire and run up to me and wag his tail but it never happened. And then when we were walking on the Strip to go to some of the places, I looked at the people walking toward us in the other direction and some of them looked scared and nervous and I could see Carl Sagan's face in their faces.

I asked Zed has he ever felt anything like that and then his face reminded me of Carl Sagan too, and even though Zed's talking again, he just nodded.

I'm not mad at Steve anymore. He's been trying really hard to find Carl Sagan, and it was his idea to make the posters in the first place. After we looked for Carl Sagan some more Steve said how about let's have lunch, it's his treat, and I said, How can you even think about eating when Carl Sagan is out there somewhere probably starving! I said we should go back to Office Depot and print out more posters and put those up too, but then Zed said that Steve's right, we already skipped breakfast, and we should eat because then we'll have more energy to look for Carl Sagan.

When Zed said that, I realized that my stomach did feel kind of empty. I said OK, fine, how about let's go to Johnny Rockets then? but Steve said he has an even better idea. He said he's going to take us to a hotel and casino called the Bellagio to eat at a Michelin-star restaurant, that'll definitely cheer me up. I asked him what's a Michelin star, is it a famous racecar driver? and Steve said it's not. He said that the Michelin people know a lot about food and they rate the best restaurants every year and the most you can get is three stars. I said in that case why don't we eat at a place that has two or three Michelin stars, and Steve said those places all need reservations way ahead of time and they have a dress code and there's no way they'd let in Zed wearing sandals. Steve said the food at the place he's taking us is going to be way better than Johnny Rockets anyway and I'll love it, he guarantees it.

The food was just so-so. We had a Chef's Lunch Tasting which means that there are five courses and the chef orders for you. The waiter asked us do we have any food allergies or is there anything we can't eat and Zed said he's vegan, and I said, Do you guys have apple pie à la mode?

Steve gave me a weird look when I said that. He said they don't have that here, it's going to be whatever the pastry chef decides and it's going to be a lot better than apple pie à la mode, and he told the waiter don't worry about it.

But then Steve was wrong! For dessert I got an apple pie à la mode except it was deconstructed, meaning the crust looked like dirt and the ice cream looked like a lake and there were no apples, just apple foam that disappeared as soon as I put it in my mouth. It was so weird.

Steve thought all our food was so good but I like Johnny Rockets better to be honest. He said I didn't like it as much because my palate isn't refined enough, and I told him, No, I didn't like it because I just didn't like it. Steve took pictures of everything we ate and he said he's going to leave a five-star review on Yelp, him and his girlfriend leave reviews on Yelp all the time, and I tried to be brave again because I thought about Carl Sagan yelping behind a dumpster or trying to cross one of the huge busy roads here in Las Vegas and yelping because he's too scared to cross.

Right after we finished our food Steve's girlfriend called and he went in the hallway to talk to her, and when he came back he was kind of mad again. I think maybe he's not in love with his girlfriend after all because if he is, then why does he get mad every time he talks to her? Then the waiter came and asked us would we like any coffee or tea and Steve said, No, just the check. And I called animal control to check on Carl Sagan and they said they still haven't seen him, and then my stomach felt empty again but I don't think it was because I was hungry.

Steve said if we don't find Carl Sagan by this afternoon we should just keep driving to LA because we've done all we can, and besides, he just promised his girlfriend he'd be back home tonight. I said, How can you say that! We haven't even looked in half of Las Vegas yet, and I know because Zed and me saw it from the top of the Stratosphere and it's huge, it's even bigger than Zed remembers! Then Steve said we can't stay here forever, and I said I'll stay here as long as I need to to find Carl Sagan, and then I remembered my maybe dad and I said, How about we go to the address we found for him because he probably knows Las Vegas a lot better than we do because he lives here.

Steve and Zed looked at each other, and Steve said, Isn't that a little too much? And I said, Too much what? And Zed said, We can always use an extra pair of eyes, and he kept staring at Steve, it was almost like he was trying to communicate with Steve telepathically. Then Steve looked back at me and he said, OK, let's go see, so we left the restaurant and I put in the address on Google Maps on Steve's phone, and we came here to where my maybe dad lives.

My maybe dad's subdivision is so nice. It even has its own golf course! We drove across a path for the golf carts and we passed some houses with weird shingles and there were guys from lawnmower companies mowing the lawns, and it reminded me of Benji's subdivision except all the trees here are palm trees. The Google Maps lady told us, Your destination is on the right, so we looked on the right and then she told us, You have arrived, and the house had tan walls and a red door and we parked the car on the street and we went up to the door.

I rang the doorbell and nobody answered. I rang the doorbell again and nobody answered again, and I didn't hear any sounds coming from inside the house either. I did hear a dog barking down the street but it wasn't Carl Sagan, it was just some other dog.

We came back to the car and Steve said it's not even five p.m. so my maybe dad's probably still at work, and Zed said let's wait a little while, maybe he'll be back soon. And I said maybe he will be, or maybe my dad won a million dollars at the casino so he doesn't have to work, and he's playing golf on the golf course right now and he's going to come back driving a golf cart and he'll have a majestic beard and he'll be a little fatter than in the pictures I have of him so it's going to take me a minute to recognize him.

I wonder if he'll recognize me.

NEW RECORDING 24
11M 38S

ALEX: OK, I started it.

UNIDENTIFIED FEMALE: You want me to just . . . talk to them?

ALEX: Yeah! Make sure you don't cover the hole on the earphone wire though.

UNIDENTIFIED FEMALE: Um, hello, beings from outer space?

UNIDENTIFIED FEMALE: I . . . I don't know what to say.

ALEX: Say your name!

UNIDENTIFIED FEMALE: My name's Terra. It's nice to meet you, sort of.

ALEX: Tell them who you are.

TERRA: I'm Alex's . . .

ALEX: She's my sister!

TERRA: Half sister. Sorry if I'm a little tongue-tied . . . I just found out that Alex and I . . . It's no small . . .

TERRA: Here, you take it. You're better than me at this.

ALEX: It's OK. You did good, sister!

TERRA: Can we please not use that word right now? Just call me Terra.

ALEX: Sure sis—I mean Terra.

TERRA: Thanks.

ALEX: Is it OK if I tell them about how we figured out I'm your half brother and you're my Terra?

TERRA: Sure.

ALEX: OK. So we were waiting in front of the house and then Terra's car pulled into the driveway, except I didn't know her name was Terra yet and I didn't know we had the same dad yet. We saw her get out of the car and Zed and me went up to her and she said, I'm sorry, we're not buying any more fund-raiser candy. I told her I'm not selling any candy, I tried that in fifth grade and it wasn't worth it. I asked her, Does someone named Joseph David Petroski live here? and she said No, he doesn't, and I said, Oh, OK, we're sorry for bothering you.

I thought maybe I put in the address wrong and we came to the wrong house, but when I turned around to go back to the car, Terra said, Wait, what do you want with Joseph David Petroski? And I said, Do you know him? And Terra said he's her father but he died eight years ago. I said, That's funny, because my dad died eight years ago when I was three and his name was

Joseph David Petroski too and he has the same birthday, and then she looked back and forth between me and Zed and she said, Is this some kind of joke?

I said, It's not a joke but do you know any good astronomy jokes? and Terra said, No, you're mistaking him for someone else, and then I got out the picture of my family from my wallet and I showed it to Terra, and I asked her, Is this him?

Terra looked at the picture and she said, Where did you get this? and I said I got it from my house. Terra looked at me and then she looked at Zed, and Zed told her she should talk with me alone for a little while, him and Steve will wait outside.

I came with Terra into the house, which has really soft carpet and walls that are yellow like mustard, and the whole place smells like air freshener. We walked by the stairs and down the hallway into the living room, and Terra told me to sit down, she'll be right back, and I heard her go upstairs. I sat down and the sofa was really comfortable and I wished Carl Sagan was there because he'd be really nervous about meeting Terra at first, but then he'd be friendlier once he got to know her, and then he'd be excited to take a nap on the sofa. And then Terra came back downstairs and she asked me what's wrong, and I told her I'm trying to be brave.

Terra sat down next to me and showed me some

pictures that were in a shoebox, and my dad was in the pictures and he looked exactly like he does in the pictures at my house except instead of with me and my mom and Ronnie he's with Terra and her mom, he's even wearing the same clothes in some of them, and that's what I told Terra.

And then Terra, who I still didn't know was Terra because I didn't ask her What's your name? yet, looked at me for a long time, and then she got out her phone. I asked her, Who are you calling? and she said she's calling her mom, but she didn't get up and go out of the room to make the call like Steve or Ronnie does, she just stayed sitting down right next to me which I liked.

She said into the phone, There's a twelve-year-old boy here at the house, and I said Eleven, and she said, Sorry, eleven-year-old boy here from Colorado and he showed me a picture of Dad. Terra's mom said something but I couldn't hear what, and she was talking for a long time because Terra was listening for a long time, and then Terra hung up the phone without even saying good-bye. Then she started crying and saying stuff but she wasn't making any sense, it runs in the family, and I started crying a little too. I just don't like seeing other people cry, I guess.

Terra stopped crying and then I stopped crying, and we just sat on the sofa and I looked at the fireplace, which had no wood in it. I asked Terra, What's your name and how old are you? and she said it's Terra and she's nineteen. I said, Terra's a really pretty name, how do you spell it? and she said T-E-R-R-A. I said, Did you know that *Terra* means Earth and my all-time hero Dr. Carl Sagan talked about TERRAforming Venus and Mars, which means making them more habitable for humans and plants and pups, and I'm recording sounds on my Golden iPod to show the intelligent beings out there what Earth is like and I went to SHARF in New Mexico to launch my iPod into space but my rocket failed, but I met Steve and Zed and made a lot of new friends and now I'm going to redouble my efforts for Voyager 4 like Lander Civet told everyone at CivSpace, and I was supposed to go back to Rockview but I got the e-mail from Ancestry.com about my dad who's also your dad so I came to Las Vegas to see if he was still alive but this was when I still thought that he had amnesia, and me and Zed went to the top of the Stratosphere and then we met Steve at Zelda's because he left the restaurant bar after he did his personal business but when we got there my dog and best non-human friend Carl Sagan was gone.

Terra looked at me and she said, What? and then she started laughing all of a sudden, and her snot was all over her face and mouth, and I started laughing even though

I didn't know what was so funny. I guess her snot was pretty funny. After we both had a good laugh, Terra went to the kitchen and she came back with some napkins that we used to wipe our faces, and I told Terra more about how we lost Carl Sagan and how I thought my maybe dad could help us look for him but now that that's not possible can SHE help us look for him?

Terra said she'll help look but not right now. She said her mom's getting home soon and we should talk to her first, and it'll be better if the guys aren't here for that. She asked me do they have anywhere else they can go, and I said they can probably go to the restaurant bar because Steve can do his personal business there and Zed can meditate anywhere, or they could go to Zelda's again because Steve really likes that place. She said that sounds good and we went outside to tell the guys, and I introduced them to Terra and told them she was my Terra except I said the other word she doesn't want me to use right now.

I think Steve was really surprised that I had a Terra. The whole time he was staring at her and his mouth was open a little and he was barely talking. I said, Hey Steve, did you turn into Zed? and he said Sorry, and I said, Can you give Terra your phone number so we can text you later after we talk with her mom? He gave it to her and then him and Zed left, and me and Terra came back inside the house, and now we're upstairs in her bedroom making this recording.

ALEX: Is that a good description of what happened, Terra?

TERRA: Alex, you're amazing.

ALEX: Terra?

TERRA: What is it?

ALEX: Why are there so many pictures of you in your room?

TERRA: Pretty embarrassing, right? It's all my mom's doing.

TERRA: But whatever, I don't live here anymore, I just come home for dinner sometimes.

ALEX: You look so pretty in them. Your hair was a lot longer.

TERRA: Alex . . .

TERRA: Listen, when she gets home I want—

[garage door opening]

TERRA: That's her. Just stay here until I come get you, OK?

ALEX: OK.

[footsteps on stairs]

ALEX: I wonder if Terra's mom wears flower dresses like my mom, because in some of the pictures that Terra showed me, she was—

[muffled shouting]

ALEX: Um . . . Terra?

[footsteps on stairs]

TERRA'S MOTHER: —*didn't want to upset you.*

TERRA: Well, that clearly worked out.

TERRA'S MOTHER: Honey, it's not that Howard and I were trying to keep—

TERRA: Wait, Howard? Howard. Howard has a say in this but I don't. I can't—

ALEX: Um . . .

TERRA: Alex, stay back.

TERRA'S MOTHER: Where's his mother? Is she here?

TERRA: No, she isn't here. He came by himself.

TERRA'S MOTHER: Hi sweetie, how did you get all the way here from—

TERRA: Don't baby-talk him. Why do you have to—

TERRA'S MOTHER: Terra, we have to get him home to his mother. He must be scared to—

TERRA: He's not some helpless little thing! Stop treating him like—

[Alex crying]

TERRA'S MOTHER: I'm sorry dear, is all the shouting making you—

TERRA: Stop it, Donna. You always do this.

TERRA'S MOTHER: Do what? What am I doing, honey?

TERRA: Just . . . stop. STOP.

TERRA: Alex, grab your stuff.

TERRA'S MOTHER: Terra, be reasonable—

TERRA: Let's go. Come on.

TERRA'S MOTHER: Talk to me, Terra. Why are you like this?

TERRA: ALEX.

[footsteps on stairs]

TERRA'S MOTHER (distant): *Terra, honey, why can't we have—*

TERRA: Just pick them up. You can put them on in the car.

[front door slamming]

TERRA: I'm sorry about all of this.

[keys jingling]

TERRA: Inside. Go.

[car doors slamming]

[engine starting]

[electronic music]

NEW RECORDING 25
11M 28S

Hi guys! This is the second time I've been in an apartment. I went to Paul Chung's apartment for a sleepover when we were friends in fourth grade and it was nicer than my house! It had clean walls and wood floors so I thought all apartments were like that, but I guess not because Terra's apartment is a lot different. It's a lot smaller and darker and some of the blinds were bent when we came in, so I went and unbent them and opened the blinds. But even with the blinds all the way open it's still kind of dark.

I told Terra, It's so weird that all the hallways and stairs of your apartment building are outdoors, and I asked her where's her basement because I need to do my laundry because I only packed enough clothes for SHARF and now they're all dirty. I told her that since she has a lot of dirty clothes all over the floor I can put our clothes in the washing machine together, but Terra said it's nonsense because I'm her guest.

She started picking up her clothes and she said the building doesn't have a basement but it does have a laundry room downstairs with machines that take quarters. I said, Oh, you mean like a slot machine, and Terra said they're like the lamest slot machines ever, because even if you're lucky the only thing you win is clean clothes.

I gave Terra all my shirts and my underwear except the underwear I was wearing, and I gave her my socks and turtleneck and told her, Make sure you wash it separate from the whites in cold water and tumble dry low. She gave me one of her T-shirts to wear that said NIRVANA and it fit me pretty good, a lot better than my K&H shirt because Terra is skinny. I asked Terra does she believe in nirvana and she said she does, and then she said, You listen to Nirvana? and I said, What do you mean, I thought it was an imaginary place where everything's perfect! She said Nirvana is also the name of a band she likes, and she played it for me on her laptop. I told her it sounds interesting but I prefer classical music and Chuck Berry.

Terra went downstairs to do our laundry and I got really hungry, that Chef's Tasting Menu I had for lunch didn't fill me up at all. I thought Terra might be hungry too and I wanted to make something for us, but when I looked in the refrigerator all she had in there was beer and ketchup and strawberry jam. She didn't have any bread either, so I couldn't even make strawberry jam sandwiches.

Terra came back from the laundry room and I asked her, Why don't you have any food in your refrigerator? and she said she usually orders delivery or she brings home food from her job as a waitress. I asked her, Where do you work? and she said a place called Domino Grill. I asked her, Is Domino Grill like Johnny Rockets because Johnny Rockets is my favorite restaurant on Earth, and she said it's a bar and grill, so they have burgers but steaks and fish too, and everything's more expensive.

Terra asked me what do I want to eat and I said can we go to Domino Grill because I want to see where my Terra works, and she said let's stay here tonight, we can order delivery, and she showed me a website on her laptop that has all these restaurants you can order from. I said, Aye yai yai, there are so many restaurants on here, I can't decide! and I asked her can we order something for Steve and Zed also and can they come over, and Terra said sure so I called Steve and I said, Hey Steve, Terra said you guys can come to her apartment and we're going to order food and do you guys want any? Steve said just order whatever as long as there's something vegan for Zed and he'll pay for all of it, and text over the address. So I asked Terra what's her address and I texted it to Steve.

We ordered Indian food because I've never tried it and there's a first time for everything. We went outside to wait for it and for Steve and Zed, and we sat down on the stairs, and it was still pretty hot out and I could only see two stars in the sky. I asked Terra how long is it going to take our food to get here and she said probably twenty minutes, and I asked her how long has she been living in her apartment and she said just about a year, and I asked her why does she call her mom and stepdad by their first names and she told me I'm full of questions. I said, Of course I'm full of questions, how can I find out the truth about stuff if I don't ask questions, DUH!

Terra laughed and she asked me what's my mom like, and I told her my mom has black hair that's starting to turn gray and her eyes are dark brown like mine. Terra's eyes aren't brown, they're green like Ronnie's and like the leaves on the trees on my street when it's cloudy. Terra's really pretty but she doesn't wear a lot of makeup like some of the girls at my school. She has natural beauty. She reminds me of Dr. Arroway except she has brown hair, not blond hair, and it's a lot shorter, like a boy's.

Terra asked me what's my house in Rockview like and what's my street like and about Ronnie and do I remember anything about our dad. Terra's full of questions too, it runs in the family.

I told her that everything I remember about our dad is what other people told me, and I told her about how him and my mom met and fell in love on the top of Mount Sam. I asked Terra how did he meet her mom, and she said she doesn't know, she never asked. She said he was never really in her life either, and he never lived with them, she's not sure why his name showed up with their address. I told her I'm not sure either, but I'm glad it did.

We went back inside after a while and then the guys got here and so did our Indian food, and we sat on the floor and spread out all the food in front of us and ripped open the paper delivery bags and used those as placemats because Terra only has two chairs for her table.

The food looked like barf but it tasted pretty good. I love the samosas and I love the bread, which is called naan. You dip it in the curry and I finished my naan and there was still a lot of curry left, and Terra said I could have her naan. I can eat a billion naans but not literally a billion, it's just an expression. Literally I can probably eat two and a half naans. I told Terra the naan was so good, and the next time we order Indian food, we should get naan à la mode.

The whole time we were eating Steve was acting really weird again. He wasn't as mad and his phone kept buzzing but he didn't even notice it, and any time Terra said something Steve would nod his head and say Yeah, Uh-huh, or I see your point. And he kept staring at Terra especially when her and Zed were talking about Zed's trip to India to find the guru. Then Terra got up to go move our clothes from the washers to the dryers and Steve got up too, and I thought he was going to the kitchen to refill his water but then he sat back down right away, I think he was just being polite because Terra was leaving her seat. Steve's quite a gentleman.

After a while I started feeling hot and stuffy all of a sudden even though the windows were open, so I went outside to look for Terra and help her with our laundry. The air outside wasn't that much cooler though, and I looked up again and I could still only see a couple of stars and then something smelled like garbage, and I remembered that Carl Sagan was still missing.

Terra came back from the laundry room and I guess she saw me sitting on the stairs crying again. She asked me what's the matter, and I said Carl Sagan hasn't even been gone for a day and I already forgot about him, I'm the worst best friend on Earth.

Terra said that doesn't make me a bad friend, it's the opposite actually, the fact that I feel guilty about not thinking about him shows how much I care. She gave me a really good hug and said we'll look for him together first thing in the morning, and then she asked me can she listen to the recordings I made for you guys on this Golden iPod. I said, Of course you can, you're my Terra so my Golden iPod is your Golden iPod, and we went back inside and she went into her room to listen to them.

While she was in her room I finished the rest of the Indian food with the guys, and then Zed was sitting on the floor meditating again and Steve went to his car and got all the phones he bought from people who needed money for an emergency. He started cleaning the phones because he's going to sell them on eBay and I said, Hey Steve, didn't you promise your girlfriend you'd be back in LA by tonight because you guys should probably get going. But Steve said it's only a five-hour drive, so they can still stay for a while.

Terra was in her room for a really long time. I thought maybe she fell asleep so I went into her room to check, and she was sitting on her bed and she had in my earphones. I told her, I'm glad you didn't fall asleep, I just wanted to make sure, and I wanted to see your face, and I think our laundry's done, but I'll come back when you're finished listening. And she said, No, come here. So I went onto the bed and she gave me another really good hug. I said, What's that for? and she said, Stay here, I'm almost done, so I stayed there. Then she started laughing a little so I laughed a little, and then she put her hand over her mouth like she was trying not to say anything, and then she took out the earphones.

I asked Terra, Why are you so sad, it's making me sad, and then she hugged me again. She said she really admires what I'm doing and she hopes I keep making my recordings, and I said, Of course I'll keep making them, I'm redoubling my efforts like Lander said, and I'm not going to stop until my Golden iPod is on its way into deep space. Terra said she wants to help me with my mission however she can. She said, You and me, we need to stick together, promise me we'll do that, and I said I promise because I've never been in Boy Scouts so I can't say Scout's Honor.

We went back into the living room and I helped Terra and the guys clean up all the delivery containers and paper bag placemats and aluminum foil, and Steve was talking about how it's really late and he's so tired from going around and looking for Carl Sagan today. Terra said if him and Zed want, they can stay the night at her place on the sofa, and also she has an air mattress, and Steve said OK right away. I guess he didn't have to be back in LA tonight after all.

Terra got out the air mattress from her closet and it was in a bag that was even smaller than my duffel bag. When I saw it I said, That's it? THAT'S the air mattress? and then she unfolded it and showed me how it works. I thought it was like sleeping on air but it's not, it's sleeping on plastic, you just blow it up with air. I asked Terra, How long does it take to blow up, because I've blown up a beach ball once and it took me five minutes because I had to stop and catch my breath, and that looks a lot bigger than a beach ball. She said it doesn't take long, it comes with a motorized pump, and she showed me.

She plugged in the pump to the wall and turned on the switch and then it went *whhrrrrrrrr* and the mattress filled up with air. I said that is SO cool, they should make an air sofa and an air coffee table and an air Lay-Z-Boy and you could fit everything into your duffel bag and that way no matter where you go, you'll always be at home. I asked Terra can I sleep on the air mattress tonight and she said, It's for the guys, we're sharing my bed if that's OK with you, and I said OK.

What a day, what a day! Even though my dad isn't still alive and can't be the man in love for my Golden iPod, and even though I still haven't found Carl Sagan yet, I did find out I have a Terra and she's full of questions and doesn't make sense when she cries and she has green eyes and I love her. I hope I get to talk to Terra's mom and stepdad, and I hope that Terra meets my mom and Ronnie soon. I'm still not sure how my dad had two families at the same time but I think Terra's mom might know. I think she might have some pieces to the jigsaw puzzle too, and if we all sit down without yelling or getting mad, we can figure out what happened. And then we'll have even more extra pairs of eyes to look for Carl Sagan!

We'll find him for sure.

NEW RECORDING 26
18M 34S

Hi guys. Terra was awake already when I woke up this morning, and she was listening to my iPod again. I rubbed my eyes and I said, Hey Terra, what are you doing? and she said there was a part of a recording that she wanted to listen to one more time. I asked her which part, and then she sat down on the edge of the bed, and she said she has something she wants to ask me.

Terra said that the guys are about to leave for LA, how would I feel if we drove to LA with them? I said, But what about Carl Sagan, you said last night you'd help me look for him! and Terra said we can still look for him this morning, but if we don't find him then maybe we can go see Ronnie, maybe Ronnie can help in some way. She said that while we're in LA, people here will still see my MISSING posters, and if someone finds him or if animal control gets a dog that matches his description, we'll drop everything and come right back.

I still didn't want to go at first because then I'd be even farther away from Carl Sagan. I told Terra that the worst part about all this is that I know he's out there somewhere but I don't know where he is and what he's doing, and I used to always know. We used to always be together. I asked Terra does she know how that feels? And she nodded and then she started picking at some fuzzies that were on the blanket, and I watched her pick at the fuzzies and I thought about how I do really want to see Ronnie though, and I want him to meet Terra too, and I remembered how Steve said the drive is five hours, which isn't that long because we were driving for a lot longer when we came from SHARF to Las Vegas.

I told Terra, How about we look for Carl Sagan and then decide, because maybe we'll get lucky and find him this morning and then we can bring him to LA with us because he hasn't met Ronnie yet either. Terra said sure, let's do that first, so we told the guys and they said they'd help us look too, and we all went to Zelda's again and to the restaurant bar and to some dumpsters but Carl Sagan wasn't at any of those places.

Finally I told Terra, OK, if you really think we should go to LA then let's go because I trust you, and besides, I promised you we'd stick together and a man is only as good as his word. I told her I'll try my best to be brave.

The guys are in front of us on the highway now. I'm riding in Terra's car which has rust on the bumpers, and whenever we go faster than seventy miles per hour the whole car starts shaking like a rocket reaching escape velocity. I asked Terra, Is this hunk of junk going to hold together? and she said she hopes so. I asked her why doesn't she buy a nicer car and she said she doesn't need nice things, she just needs her own things, and I respect that.

TERRA: I'm glad I have your respect, Alex.

ALEX: Hey Terra?

TERRA: Yeah?

ALEX: Did you tell your mom you're going to LA?

TERRA: Nope.

ALEX: She's your mom. You should at least tell her.

TERRA: I'll tell her later. She's just going to worry if I tell her right now and it's not like I need her permission anyway. I'm legally an adult. If I want to go, I'm going to go.

ALEX: Do you always yell at her like yesterday?

TERRA: I wasn't—well, no, not always.

TERRA: It's just sometimes she doesn't listen. And she treats me like I can't take care of myself. If I call her now she'll freak out, like, But where are you going to stay? What are you going to eat?

TERRA: It's like, Donna! There are *hotels* in LA. There are *restaurants*. People *live* there.

ALEX: I know what you mean. It's like when someone thinks I'm still nine or ten years old. I hate that because I'm eleven, not nine. I'm in middle school, not fourth grade. And I'm probably at least thirteen in responsibility years!

TERRA: It's a big difference, isn't it? They just don't get it.

ALEX: They just don't get it.

TERRA: I don't know what happened though, it wasn't always like this.

ALEX: Like what?

TERRA: With my mom. Our relationship was a lot different. I used to tell her everything. If there was . . . something I'd done that I knew she wouldn't approve of—like, some hard decision that I'd made on my own, I'd tell her about it afterwards. And I felt that at least she understood why I made the choices I did, even if she wasn't always happy about them.

ALEX: Was one of the choices to move to your own apartment? She wasn't happy probably because she knew she was going to really miss you.

TERRA: Mmm . . . yeah, I guess. But it's just that sometimes parents don't want to accept that their kids are growing up. It's like they think, I don't know, they think if we grow up, then we stop being their kids or something. But that's their whole job! It's to raise us to be independent! They just have such a hard time facing it, you know? Facing the truth.

ALEX: My hero believed in the truth.

TERRA: I remember that from your recordings. I believe in it too. And anyway, my point is that at least back then I felt like Donna listened, and respected my ability to make my own choices. But somewhere over the last few years she started getting like this and—

TERRA: Sorry. I don't mean to be dumping all this on you.

[phone chiming]

ALEX: Terra, don't.

TERRA: Don't what?

ALEX: Don't text and drive at the same time. We could get into an accident.

TERRA: You're very considerate.

TERRA: I'll tell you what—you take the phone.

ALEX: Me?

TERRA: Yup. You don't want me to text, right? So you'll have to be my eyes and fingers.

ALEX: OK! Let me put down my iPod—

[rustling]

TERRA: Here, the cup holder—

ALEX: This thing—

TERRA: I'll move the—

ALEX: I got it.

TERRA: Great. Now read me the text.

ALEX: It's from Amy Carter. She says she can cover for you while you're gone.

TERRA: Tell her thanks, I owe her one.

[keys clicking]

[phone chiming]

ALEX: She says, I guess this means you're not going to Jordan's party tonight?

TERRA: That's right.

[phone chiming]

TERRA: What'd she say?

ALEX: It's someone else this time. Terra, you're really popular.

TERRA (laughing): Who is it now?

ALEX: It's Brandon Mullen. He says, Hey.

ALEX: Is he your boyfriend?

TERRA: No, we're not—well, maybe. Not really.

ALEX: Did you guys kiss already?

TERRA: We did a little more than that.

ALEX: You mean you French-kissed?

TERRA: Yes. We French-kissed.

ALEX: Then you're girlfriend and boyfriend.

TERRA (laughing): It's so simple. I don't know why we overcomplicate things.

TERRA: It's just a fling.

ALEX: What did you fling?

TERRA: A fling's when two people love each other for a really short time and then they go their separate ways.

ALEX: Oh, I had a fling too.

TERRA: You did?

ALEX: Yup. At the start of fourth grade there was a girl in my class named Emily Madsen who was a can-can dancer for Halloween, and we sat together at lunch and swinged on the swings at recess and then her family moved to North Carolina and I never saw her again.

TERRA: Now there's a fling if I ever heard of one.

ALEX: It's for the best though, we were both too young and she's not really my type anyway.

TERRA: I didn't know you had a type.

ALEX: Of course I have a type, DUH! Don't you have a type?

TERRA: Maybe. What's your type?

ALEX: Someone like Dr. Judith Bloomington. She's a professor of astrophysics at Cornell University and she's written dozens of research papers and five books on becoming a multi-planetary species and a book of short stories and poetry also, and she's kind and sweet and beautiful and she's forty-nine years old.

TERRA: She sounds like quite a woman.

[phone chiming]

ALEX: It's Brandon again. He says, Can't stop thinking about you.

TERRA: Text him back.

ALEX: What should I text him?

TERRA: Whatever you want. My phone is your phone.

ALEX: OK.

[keys clicking]

[phone chiming]

[keys clicking]

[phone chiming]

[keys clicking]

TERRA: What'd you say?

ALEX: I said, Hi Brandon, do you know any astronomy jokes?

[phone chiming]

TERRA: And he said . . .

ALEX: He said, Was your daddy a thief?

ALEX: And then I said, No, he was a civil engineer.

ALEX: And then he said, I think he was a thief, 'cause he stole the stars and put them in your eyes.

ALEX: And then I said, No, I'm pretty sure he was a civil engineer, and I told him you can't steal the stars because even the closest ones are trillions of miles away and nobody owns them.

[Terra laughing]

[phone chiming]

ALEX: He says, I like it when you play hard to get.

[phone chiming]

ALEX: He says, What are you wearing?

[keys clicking]

ALEX: I told him I'm wearing your NIRVANA shirt.

[phone chiming]

ALEX: He says, Wait, who is this?

[Terra laughing]

[keys clicking]

[phone chiming]

[phone chiming]

[keys clicking]

ALEX: He says, Who's Alex? Where's Terra? It's in all capital letters.

ALEX: I said, Hi Brandon, I think your caps-lock is broken.

[Terra laughing]

[phone ringing]

ALEX: He's calling now.

TERRA: Let it go to voicemail.

ALEX: OK.

TERRA: Well done. You're in charge of the phone from now on.

ALEX: In charge of the phone! In charge of the phone!

ALEX: Hey Terra?

TERRA: Yeah?

ALEX: Why aren't you in college? You're nineteen. You're supposed to be in college.

TERRA: You sound like my mom.

ALEX: I do?

TERRA: It's a long story.

ALEX: We have time, Google Maps says it's going to be another four hours before we get to LA. Did you drop out of school?

TERRA: I didn't drop out. I just didn't want to go in the first place.

ALEX: Why not? My hero went to college. He went to lots of colleges. First he went to the University of Chicago and got his bachelor's and master's and PhDs in astronomy and astrophysics and then he lectured at Harvard and then he became a professor at Cornell University in Ithaca, New York.

TERRA: Your hero didn't have my mom and Howard.

ALEX: He had Rachel and Sam Sagan.

TERRA: And I bet they were nothing like my mom and Howard. When I was a little older than you—when I was thirteen—I realized that as soon as I was eighteen I was going to move out of the house. So when I turned eighteen, that's what I did.

ALEX: But then why didn't you go to college? You still could've gone.

TERRA: I could have, but I know people who got their degrees but then couldn't find work when they graduated. I mean, most of the stuff they teach you there doesn't prepare you for a real-world job, which is the whole point anyway, so why go hundreds of thousands of dollars in debt when you're just competing against other people on an artificial standard or even worse, drinking and partying away four years of your life only to come out with a piece of paper that isn't worth sh—

TERRA: Sorry, I just get really mad about it sometimes.

ALEX: It's OK, I know all the swear words.

TERRA: Oh yeah?

ALEX: Yeah. One time in school, Justin Petersen who's on the basketball team and his locker's next to mine asked me, Do you even know any swear words? And I said, Of course I do, DUH! and then I told him all the swear words and I said sometimes Benji and I even combine them into sentences like, Bleep the bleep bleep who bleeped on my bleep bleep bleeping bleeper.

TERRA: I see.

ALEX: But Terra, why does the point of college have to be to get you a job?

TERRA: Why else would you go?

ALEX: Because you're interested in knowledge.

TERRA: ——

TERRA: You know what, I take back what I said. I think some people actually get a lot out of college, and you're going to be one of them. I'm sure of it.

[phone chiming]

TERRA: Brandon again?

ALEX: It's Steve. He says, Are you guys hungry? Do you need to stop and use the bathroom?

[phone chiming]

ALEX: He says, Let me know, smiley face.

TERRA: I could wait till we get to LA. What do you think?

ALEX: Can we go to Johnny Rockets when we get there?

TERRA: Sure.

[keys clicking]

[phone chiming]

ALEX: Steve says we should go to In-N-Out because it's way better, hamburger French fry thumbs-up.

[keys clicking]

[phone chiming]

ALEX: I asked him do they have apple pie à la mode and he says they have milkshakes, cow ice-cream cone.

TERRA: The guys can go to In-N-Out if they want. I'll take you to Johnny Rockets.

ALEX: OK!

TERRA: I'm low on gas though. Tell him we're taking the next exit.

ALEX: OK.

[keys clicking]

[phone chiming]

[phone chiming]

NEW RECORDING 27
11M 52S

What an afternoon! And it's still not even over yet.

Terra and I were driving and then the freeway got wider, like five lanes instead of two, and there were more cars and everyone was going faster. We didn't listen to music and we didn't talk and Terra said she liked the silence, and I said there's not really silence, there's the sound of the wind and the road and the air conditioner, and the sound of cars passing and me talking right now, and Terra said that's very true. She said she likes the peacefulness, and I said I like it too, so we listened to the peacefulness and then I told her an astronomy joke.

I said, Why didn't the Dog Star laugh at the comedy show?

Because it was too Sirius.

Terra laughed and I said, Did you get it? because some

of the kids at school didn't get it because they thought I was talking about satellite radio. Terra said she got it, it's because Sirius is the name of a star that's also called the Dog Star, but it sounds like *serious* too, as in a serious person, and I said, That's why you're my Terra, you really get me.

Terra laughed again and we listened to the peacefulness again, and then she said she has a sudden urge to go swimming. She asked me do I want to go swimming and I said, But what about LA? and she said we'll only stop for an hour or two, it'd be nice to cool down in this heat. I said, That's a great idea because your car's air conditioner sure isn't doing that right now. Terra said there's a lake nearby that she's been to before and I looked it up on Google Maps, then I texted Steve and he said, But we'll be in LA in a couple of hours, how about we go swimming when we get there? I told him Terra wants to go swimming right now, and he said thumbs-up swimmer sun tidal wave.

We took the exit for the lake and then the road got really curvy all of a sudden, and Terra was driving SO fast. The speed limit was fifty-five miles per hour but on some of the turns you were only supposed to go twenty-five, and it was like Forza Motorsport which I watch Benji play at his house sometimes except Terra didn't do any skids. We saw the lake down the side of the cliffs and trees but we didn't see a way to get there, so we kept driving and then we saw signs that took us to the lake. At the entrance the park ranger lady said it was five dollars cash but Terra only had her credit card, so I let her borrow some money because she's family.

We got out of our cars and there were a lot of families making barbecue at the picnic tables, and some kids were throwing a tennis ball back and forth in the water, and other people down the shore had kayaks and there were babies in the shallow part with their moms and dads. The beach isn't a normal beach because there isn't regular sand, the sand is really tiny rocks instead, and we took off our shoes and our socks and put them in our shoes so we wouldn't get rock sand in them. Zed put his round pillow on the rock sand and he started meditating, and Steve started putting on sunscreen and he asked do me and Terra want any, and Terra said thanks and she helped me put sunscreen on my face and neck and shoulders. Steve asked Terra does she need any help putting on sunscreen and she said, Alex can help me, isn't that right? And I said that's right and I helped her.

We sat on the rock sand and watched the people already in the water, and the kids throwing the tennis ball were playing a game that looked like dodgeball. Except instead of throwing the ball through the air they'd try to skip it on the water a bunch of times first, it was waterdodgeball, and after a while Terra said, Let's go for a dip. Steve said we probably shouldn't because we don't have towels or swimsuits and we'll get our car seats all wet, but Terra started taking off her jean shorts anyway and went in the water in her tank top and underwear, it was a tank top bikini. Steve didn't try to stop her or anything, he just watched her splash in. And then he said, Why is it always the ones like her? but he wasn't talking to me, he was just talking out at the water. I asked him, What do you mean the ones like her? The ones like who? Like Terra? What ones like Terra? And then he said, Never mind, and I said, Hey, that's the name of an album by Nirvana the band.

Terra was yelling from the water, Alex, come on! The water's amazing! And I yelled back, What about getting your car seats wet! And then she yelled, Don't be such a Steve! and I laughed because I was totally being a Steve. I said, Hey Steve, did you put on enough sunscreen because you're already turning red, and then Terra yelled my name again and I said, Come on Steve, let's go! but he said no. I guess he was still worried about getting his seats wet. I told him it's his loss, and I took off my shirt and pants and I went in.

I couldn't do a cannonball because it was too shallow so I just belly-flopped, and the water was SO cold. Terra laughed and said that when I jumped in I looked like a small whale, and I said, That reminds me, do you know where we can see some whales because I want to record some new whale songs for my Golden iPod. Terra said she doesn't know, but we can look it up when we get to LA.

The water in the lake was really fresh and clear and dark blue-green. When I looked closely I could see tiny green dots floating in the water like the chia seed kombucha drinks Benji's mom has in their refrigerator. Terra said it's a kind of harmless algae, and I told her I've never seen algae in a lake like this, and she said, Isn't it beautiful? and I said, Yes, it's almost the color of your eyes.

We went out to where the water was a little deeper, and it was less rocky but I could barely touch the bottom on my tippy toes and there were some lakeweeds that were scratchy and they tickled my feet. Terra was floating on her back and the sun was shining off the water like diamonds, and I wished I brought my sunglasses but they're at my house in Rockview. We went out past the kids who were playing waterdodgeball and it was even deeper and I couldn't touch the bottom anymore, and Terra said to hold on to her so I did, and the water bounced up and down but there weren't any big waves that you can go surfing on. I asked Terra, Have you ever been surfing because I've never been surfing, only skateboarding, and the one time I went skateboarding I fell off and scraped my knee so I'm not doing it again until I can afford the proper protection. Terra said she hasn't been surfing either, but when we get to LA we're totally going to rent some surfboards and learn by ourselves.

Terra loves the water. She said she doesn't spend enough time in it. She said whenever she gets in a lake or an ocean, it feels like she's returned to the earth. I said, That makes no sense because you never left the earth, and she said it's just an expression, it's more like when she's in the water she feels like she's in her most natural environment. I said, Oh, that makes a lot more sense, because we originally evolved from colonies of bacteria in the ocean hundreds of millions of years ago. I told her also our bodies are made mostly of water, so if you think about it, it's like if you fill up a water balloon and put it in a bathtub full of water, then the only thing that keeps the inside water separate from the outside water is the skin of the balloon, and if the skin wasn't there there'd really be no difference. Terra said that's very deep, and I told her you can do it in a sink too, it doesn't have to be as deep as a bathtub.

I think Steve saw all the fun me and Terra were having and got jealous because he finally came out in the water too. He took off his shirt but kept on his shorts, and he stepped in little by little and splashed some water on himself to get used to how cold it was. Terra and I went back to the shallower part by Steve where the water came up just to my neck, and Terra could stand on her knees, and if you didn't know that Terra was standing on her knees and you saw us, it probably looked like we were the same height. Steve got down on his knees too, and when he finally came all the way into the water he looked so happy. I said, See Steve? We told you it was a good idea to come out. And Steve said he's glad he did.

We swam over to the kids who were playing water-dodgeball and asked them, Can we play? and they said yes. Terra and I went to where the kids were on one side and Steve stayed with the rest of the kids on the other side, and we played waterdodgeball and it was so much fun. Those kids could throw the ball SO far and fast. I tried to throw it hard but it didn't go as far and fast, but the other kids were really good at skipping it on the water, and the ball would curve and spin and go *puu puu puu* away from where you thought it was going. When it was Steve's turn he threw the ball really REALLY hard to Terra, and it skipped on the water a bunch of times and hit her in the mouth! She put her hands over her mouth and she said Ow! and then she started going toward the shore. Everyone asked her, Are you OK? Especially Steve, and she said she's OK, she's just going to the bathroom. Steve got out too and he kept saying he's sorry, he didn't mean to, and Terra said it's OK, it was an accident. Steve looked really disappointed afterwards and I said, Hey Steve, don't be so down on yourself, it was an accident! I told him to come back in the water, we're still not done with our game yet, but Steve said he doesn't feel like it anymore. He said he's going to call his girlfriend, and I should go back over by Zed because I shouldn't be in the water if nobody's watching me, so I said good-bye to the kids and I told them it was fun playing with them.

I watched Steve walk along the shore and I let the sun dry the water on me, and pretty soon I was dry except for my hair and underwear. And I was waiting for Terra to come back from the bathroom so I thought it might be a good time to learn how to meditate. I said, Hey Zed, I don't mean to interrupt but can you teach me how to meditate because I want to learn how to do it right. He said sure, he can teach me, so I sat down and I put my hands in my lap like I was pretend-holding a cheeseburger the way Zed was doing, and I squinted my eyes and told him, OK, I'm ready.

Zed said that I should focus on my breathing, and let all my thoughts go out of my head as the breath goes out of my lungs, and I said that's physically impossible because our brains are always thinking something. Zed said to look for the gap between the thoughts and I tried and I couldn't find it, because as soon as I'm done with one thought I have another, like how when Zed said the word *gap* I thought of the gap between Ken Russell's teeth, and as soon as I stopped thinking about that I thought about how we came all the way here from SHARF and now I have a Terra to help me make my recordings, and then I thought about my wet hair and underwear and then about Carl Sagan, and then I wanted to call animal control again.

Zed said that's great, just notice yourself thinking, and look for that moment when nothing seems to exist, not even time. I said, Oh, you mean like in a black hole, because in a black hole the gravity is so strong that it bends light and time and space. Zed said that's a great metaphor, and I said, Thanks, feel free to use it in your next book.

So then I closed my eyes and I tried to imagine myself in a black hole, and after a while I started seeing colors. First I saw the red color that you see when you look at the sun with your eyes closed, but then I saw pinks and blues and they were in blobby shapes and it was almost like in *Contact* when Dr. Arroway looks out the transporter window and sees the swirling galaxy and she says, So . . . beautiful . . . no . . . words . . . they should've sent . . . a poet.

I think I fell asleep even, but I'm not sure, and when I opened my eyes I saw the beach, except it wasn't the cosmic beach like in *Contact* and there wasn't a super-intelligent being speaking to me through a form that looked and sounded like my dad. There was just the rock sand beach of this lake in California and there was Zed who was meditating next to me, and he's still here right now, and Terra's still not back yet from the bathroom and Steve's not back yet from his walk.

I wonder if Ronnie's ever been swimming in this lake. I bet when we get to LA in a couple of hours we'll go to his place and he'll open the door, and I'll say, SURPRISE! and he'll say, What are you doing here! and I'll run at him and hug him and he'll hug me back and he'll say, Why is your hair wet? and I'll say, I went swimming in a lake, and then he'll notice someone behind me and he'll say, Who's this? and I'll tell him she's our Terra and she lives in Las Vegas and Look, she has eyes just like yours.

I can't wait to see Ronnie's face when I tell him that.

NEW RECORDING 28
12M 34S

Guess where we are, guys . . .

We're in LA!

Guess where in LA we are . . .

We're at Johnny Rockets!

It's just me and Terra here though. Steve went to have dinner with his girlfriend, and Zed's back at the apartment, and I finally met their other roommate Nathan! Nathan's really tall and skinny. He was sitting under some palm trees in their courtyard and drinking an iced coffee when we got there, and when him and Zed stood next to each other they looked like C-3PO and R2-D2, except Nathan has blond hair down to his chin and not as good posture and he wears glasses and his skin isn't gold. I guess he's not really like C-3PO.

The guys's apartment is way nicer than Terra's apartment, by the way. It's even nicer than Paul Chung's! It's on the third floor and the outside hallway looks over the courtyard, and their living room has big windows at the end that take up the whole wall, it's a sightseer living room. When we walked in I saw a bunch of empty boxes in the corner and padded envelopes and big rolls of bubble tape, which I popped. There were also twenty sealed boxes of Battlemorphs booster packs—I've never seen so many Battlemorph cards in my whole life!

I said, Hey Steve, you must love Battlemorphs even more than Benji does, and Steve said it's another one of his side adventures. He showed me how he opens the boxes and takes out all the packs, and then he weighs them one by one on a scale like the one Benji's mom has in their kitchen. Steve said he can tell without opening them which packs have holograms because the packs with holograms weigh a little more than the ones without holograms. He said he opens the hologram packs and sells the hologram cards by themselves, especially the ultra-rares, and then he keeps the not-hologram packs sealed and sells those too because people don't want to buy packs that are already open. See, guys? I told you Steve was entrepreneurial.

I wanted to e-mail Benji and tell him about Steve's side adventure but I wanted to go surprise Ronnie too, so I told Terra let's go to Ronnie's place ASAP. Steve said he's leaving also, he's having dinner with his girlfriend and he'll probably just sleep over at her place tonight, so if Terra and me want we can stay in his room. Terra said thanks for the offer but we should go talk to Ronnie first, then we can figure it out.

I called Ronnie and it went to his voicemail, so I left him a message and I said, Hey Ronnie, I hope you're not too busy because I have a couple of surprises for you! And then Terra said, He's not home? and I told her sometimes he just puts his phone on silent, you never know with Ronnie. I said we should go there anyway and ring his doorbell, and Terra said OK.

I put in Ronnie's address in Google Maps and we followed the directions, and it took even longer to get there than the Google Maps lady told us, we kept getting stuck in traffic jams because there are SO many cars in LA. There are so many palm trees here too, and they're even taller than the ones I saw in Las Vegas! Then finally we got to Ronnie's place and we went up to the gate but I didn't have his condo number, I didn't even know it was a condo until Terra pointed at the sign in front that said *Residence West Condominiums*.

I called Ronnie again and this time he answered. I said, Hey Ronnie, are you at home right now and what's your condo number and why didn't you tell me you live in a condo? and Ronnie said he's not home right now, he's in Detroit for a prospective client's high school basketball showcase. I said, When are you coming back from Detroit because I'm standing here in front of your Residence West Condominiums and there's someone I want you to meet, and Ronnie said, What are you talking about? You're in LA?

I told him, That's right, we came here with Steve and Zed who I met at SHARF, but first they took me to Las Vegas to see about our maybe dad and he was our real dad except he didn't get amnesia and isn't still alive, and we lost Carl Sagan at Zelda's and I've been trying to be brave and then I met Terra who's your Terra also, and we went swimming in a lake and then we came to LA and I didn't tell you we were coming because I wanted to surprise you.

Ronnie said, What! Who said you could do any of that! And I said, You did! You just weren't paying attention! and Ronnie said, I can't believe you did that! And then he said we have a major problem because he's in Detroit for another few days, and then I thought that maybe it wasn't such a great idea to try and surprise Ronnie.

Ronnie said he'll call Lauren right away and I can get the spare keys from her and stay at his place tonight until he can figure something out, and I told him, That's OK, we already have a room to stay in because Steve's going to have a sleepover at his girlfriend's after they have dinner, and Ronnie said, Who? and I said, Steve, I already told you I met him and Zed at SHARF, remember? And then Terra asked to see the phone.

Terra and Ronnie talked for a while, and I heard Terra say that she's a friend and he can trust her, he can look her up on Facebook if he doesn't. I think she calmed down Ronnie, because Ronnie wasn't yelling anymore after Terra gave the phone back to me, although he still sounded mad. He told me just stay with Terra until he gets home and call him if there's any trouble at all, and he gave me Lauren's phone number too. Ronnie said he's going to talk to our mom about all this, and I told him OK, but she's been having her quiet days again.

After we talked to Ronnie, I asked Terra, Why didn't you tell Ronnie you're our half-you-know-what? Just because I promised I wouldn't use that word doesn't mean you can't use it. And Terra said these things are better handled in person. I said, Look what happened when we tried to handle it in person with your mom, and Terra said touché. I asked her what does touché mean and she told me it's French meaning You Have a Good Point.

We went back to the car and Terra wasn't talking and I didn't feel like talking either, so we didn't talk, we just sat in the car. Except this time there wasn't peacefulness and I didn't like listening to it. And then Terra asked me what's wrong, is it Carl Sagan again? and I said, It is, but it's also that I told my mom I was going to be back after

SHARF but I wasn't, and then I told her I was going to be back after Las Vegas but I wasn't either, and now we have to wait for Ronnie and I'm not being a man of my word and what if my mom finished the food I made for her and she doesn't feel like cooking by herself? Who's going to make food for her then?

And then neither of us felt like talking again and there wasn't peacefulness again.

I guess Terra didn't like listening to the not-peacefulness either because she started the car, and I said, Are we going back to the guys's place? and Terra said she doesn't know. But then she said let's go to the ocean and watch the sunset, she needs some space to think, so we went to a beach called Venice Beach. I TOLD you guys Terra loves the water. First we were in a lake and then we went to the Pacific Ocean, all in the same day.

Venice Beach was so huge, guys. I could see it even as we were driving up, and I said, Son of a beach! B-E-A-C-H. There was so much sand and it was all regular sand too, not rock sand like that lake, and it kept getting in our shoes so we took off our shoes and socks and we walked by the water's edge where the sand was wet and flat and dark brown. We went in for a while but just to our ankles, and I told Terra you can definitely surf in these waves. Every time a wave came it would pull the sand around my feet and between my toes back in little swirls. I told

Terra, Isn't it interesting how if you don't move your feet when the water comes you sink a little into the sand, and maybe if you stay in the same spot for long enough eventually the sand will come up all the way to your neck and you'll get stuck. Terra said, What if once you realize you're stuck it's too late, and all you can do then is watch yourself drown? And I said, Terra, let's keep moving because I don't want you to drown.

We kept moving and walked along the water, and there were blue lifeguard towers and yellow lifeguard trucks and people jogging and playing Frisbee with their dogs. I borrowed Terra's phone again and texted Steve, and I asked him did he get any calls from animal control about Carl Sagan? But he said he didn't.

By then the sun was getting close to the horizon so we stopped and watched it set. When it started going behind the mountains far away up the shore, I could stare at it directly, not all the time but more than during the day. Even after the sun was gone the clouds above were still bright red, and the horizon was gold and the water was purple and they should've sent a poet.

Terra and me kept moving again and we walked to the boardwalk except the ground wasn't made of wooden boards, it was made of regular cement, so it was just a cementwalk. We walked by a skateboarding park and we stopped and watched the skateboarders, and some of them had cameras on their boards and helmets like the one Skywalker team had on their rocket. We saw people Rollerblading and riding their bikes and a guy playing African drums, and we walked by a bunch of people in a circle around some shirtless guys doing gymnastics. One of the guys had a microphone and he was asking for volunteers, and the volunteers stood in a line in the middle and the other guys ran and jumped over the whole line and it was SO cool. And then we came here to Johnny Rockets because Terra promised in the car.

Terra ordered fries and coffee but she was barely eating any of her fries. I asked her, Why aren't you eating your fries and can I have some? and she said, They're all yours. She said she's just feeling a little nauseous, that's all, and I asked her does she need to see a doctor, because I know a great doctor except he's back in Rockview and his name is Dr. Turner and every year when I go for my checkup he gives me a clean bill of health, which is this pink but sometimes blue money that says *One Clean Bill of Health* and it has Dr. Turner's face instead of George Washington.

Terra said it's no big deal, thanks, she'll be better in the morning, and I said, How are you so sure? I told her if Benji was here he would probably think she's psychic or something since Benji loves the horoscope, but I don't believe in all that astrology business. Terra said she's not psychic, it's just that time of the month for her, and I asked her what time, Tuesday?

She stared at me for a little while like we were having a staring contest, so I looked into her eyes and tried not to blink except I blinked so I lost. And then she leaned in really close and she said, *I'm having my period.*

I said, Do you mean like at the end of a sentence? and Terra said it was a sentence all right, but a different kind of sentence, one that makes her bloated and ugly and want to crawl into bed. I told her, You're still beautiful to me, and I asked her is having a period like having a pop quiz, because I know some kids at school who hate pop quizzes and they start to feel sick and ask to go to the bathroom whenever we have a pop quiz. I said, But me personally, I like pop quizzes, especially in science, so maybe I'd like having a period.

Terra laughed really hard for like two minutes! And then she said, For someone so smart, you sure are clueless about a lot of things, and I said, Of course I'm clueless about a lot of things, I spend all my time learning about rockets and astronomy and my hero and if I spent my time learning about other stuff I'd be smarter about other stuff too, DUH! I said, That's why I try to surround myself with people who ARE smart about other stuff, like you, Terra.

Terra got really quiet, and she looked like she was

either going to cry or throw up or both so I asked her is it her period again. And then she went to the bathroom but she still never explained what's a period. I think it's a metaphor. Our waitress Clara came back to refill our water and I asked Clara, Do you know what's a period, is it like a pop quiz because my Terra is having her period even though it's summer and she doesn't go to college, and then Clara spilled the water on our table and she said she's so sorry and she'll be right back with some paper towels.

Why won't anyone tell me what a period is! I'm going to look it up when we get back to the guys's apartment. I'll explain it to you when I find out.

NEW RECORDING 29
6M 24S

I found out what a period is.

It's . . . um . . . not like a pop quiz.

Anyway . . .

Steve was already home when we came back to the guys's place. He was watching TV and drinking a beer on the sofa, and I said, Hey Steve, I thought you were having dinner and then a sleepover at your girlfriend's place! And he said he doesn't want to talk about it. He told us we can still stay in his room though, he'll just sleep on the sofa, and then I could hear snoring coming from one of the other rooms. I guess Zed went to bed early.

Steve asked Terra does she want a beer and she said Sure, and Nathan was drinking one too and his blond hair was tied back in a ponytail now, and he was on his laptop writing computer code. I looked on his screen and he had six windows open at the same time, and the fonts in all the windows were SO small. I don't know how he can even read anything.

Then I guess Steve really did want to talk about his dinner because after he came back with Terra's beer he said he told his girlfriend about why we didn't get back to LA until today and she yelled at him. Terra said, Why are you going out with her? and Steve said he has no idea, and then he took a big gulp of his beer. Terra opened her beer and I told everyone, I don't know how you guys can drink that stuff because I tried a sip of one of Benji's dad's beers once and it was so gross. But they kept drinking anyway, and after they ran out of beers Steve made some drinks by mixing together LOX and vodka.

When I was six years old, Ronnie had a party at our house when our mom went to the Philippines to visit Lola and Lolo, and Ronnie told me to stay in our room and he even moved the TV in there so I could watch TV. But then I had to go to the bathroom so I came out and waited by the door because it was occupied, and one of Ronnie's friends was waiting too. She was drinking from a red plastic cup and I asked her, What are you drinking? and she said it's Coke and vodka, and that's when I learned about vodka, I already knew what Coke was. Ronnie saw me and he said I'm not allowed to be out here and I need to go back to our room so I did, but I still really had to pee and I tried holding it in but I couldn't. I started crying and I guess Ronnie heard me because he came in and he asked me what's wrong. I showed him and he said, Why didn't you say something? And I said, You told me to stay in our room so I stayed in our room.

I don't know why I remembered that just now. I guess it's because of the vodka and because there was music and dancing at that party too. Terra really wanted to listen to some music, so she plugged in her phone to Steve's surround sound. I said, Shouldn't we turn it down a little? We'll wake up Zed! And Steve said that Zed can sleep through anything, he's slept through a fire alarm before, and then Steve turned up the music even louder.

Terra started dancing and she said, Come on Alex, let's dance, so I got up and I danced too. She tried to get Nathan to dance but Nathan doesn't dance, he just kept writing his tiny computer code, and Steve was sweating a lot and talking really loud and sometimes his eyes were half-open but it wasn't like he was meditating, it was more like he turned into a zombie, and then he was dancing behind Terra and she was dancing with him but she wasn't twerking, and I think Steve might like Terra but . . . doesn't he already have a girlfriend?

Steve said something to Terra and she laughed, and then she started dancing with me again. I told her I'm not that good of a dancer, I don't know how to break-dance like Paul Chung and I don't know how to twerk and Terra said I just need more practice, and she held my hands and told me to follow her feet. But her feet were kind of wobbly and when I followed her I started getting so dizzy, I had to stop after a while. Steve went to the bathroom and Terra sat down and started talking to Nathan, and then her and Nathan got up and walked toward the door and I said, Where are you guys going? and Terra said they're just going to get some fresh air, and when they left I turned down the music so it wasn't as loud.

Steve came out from the bathroom and he asked me where's Terra, and I said Terra's outside with Nathan getting some fresh air. Steve said, What! and he was still talking really loud even though I turned down the music. Then Terra and Nathan came back and Terra was laughing and Nathan was smiling, and Steve looked like he'd seen a ghost. Steve said, What took you guys so long? and Terra said they were just out there talking, and Steve turned up the music again and dimmed some of the lights too, and it kind of reminded me of when we were at Zelda's, and then . . . I don't know . . . I didn't feel like being in there anymore, so I came out here to the hallway.

Grown-ups can be so weird sometimes. Sometimes when I'm around grown-ups for too long who aren't my mom, I just want to yell, Are all of you totally crazy!

Do you ever feel like that?

Maybe you don't, because you spend your whole childhood inside your mom's belly, so when you're born you're already a full adult. Or at least you grow into an adult really quick—it doesn't take eighteen years.

Maybe you guys—

[loud music]

TERRA: Alex?

[music fading]

TERRA: What are you doing out here?

ALEX: I'm making a recording.

TERRA: Come back inside, it's not a party without you.

ALEX: I don't want to dance anymore.

TERRA: That's OK. I'm done too. Let's do something else.

ALEX: I wish I had my Blu-ray of Contact because then we could watch Contact. Have you seen it?

TERRA: I haven't, but maybe the guys have it. Or they can find it on Netflix or something.

ALEX: Really?

TERRA: Yeah, come on.

ALEX: OK!

NEW RECORDING 30
1OM 35S

Good morning, guys. We didn't get to finish *Contact* last night unfortunately. We didn't even watch half of it. Nathan went to sleep before we started so it was just me, Steve, and Terra, and Steve made microwave popcorn and he told me if at any time I feel like I can't keep my eyes open, I can go to sleep in his room and him and Terra can finish the movie by themselves. But then Terra fell asleep first!

I thought maybe Terra thought *Contact* was boring, that's why she fell asleep, but Steve said she's probably just tired from all the driving and dancing and drinks and I said touché. And then she woke up and I said, Hey Terra, do you want to go to bed now? and she nodded her head.

Terra wasn't in our bed anymore when I woke up this morning though. At first I thought she went to the bathroom or maybe she went to return to the earth again, but

I went to the bathroom to check and she wasn't there, Steve was there, and he was saying something to his reflection in the mirror. I said, Hey Steve, what are you saying to your reflection? and he said it's nothing. Steve told me to tell Terra he's going to be back later, he has something he needs to take care of, and also he's going to drop off Zed at a meditation seminar.

Zed gave me a big hug before him and Steve left. He said I'm in good hands with my Terra, and he hopes everything goes OK with Ronnie, and if he doesn't see me again before I leave he hopes I find Carl Sagan. I told him I've been trying really hard to be brave, can he tell? And he said he can definitely tell. Then him and Steve left and I started cleaning up all the dirty cups and empty beer and LOX cans lying around and putting them in a bag for recycling, and that's when I heard Terra's voice coming from Nathan's room.

I thought maybe they were French-kissing and I thought you guys might want to know what that sounds like, so I went to go record it for you. But when I got to Nathan's room they were just sitting on the floor talking. I said, Hey Terra, did you sleepwalk to Nathan's room or something and what are you guys talking about? and Terra laughed and said they were talking about all kinds of stuff. I told them I'm going to make breakfast soon and do they want some? and Terra said thanks but we don't have to do that for them. She said her and Nathan are going to talk some more and I said, OK, I'll shut the door again because I respect your privacy.

I came back out here and made breakfast and then I called Cheryl at animal control again, and she said, Hi Alex, still nothing. I said, Oh, OK . . . And then I borrowed Nathan's laptop but it was hard to concentrate because I kept thinking about Carl Sagan, and I forgot why I even went on the laptop in the first place. Then I just went onto Rocketforum.

Everyone on Rocketforum was talking about the Mars satellite mission. The launch is in three days and CivSpace is going to live-stream it like they did with their last one, and I can't wait to watch it! Skywalker team posted some pictures of Lander Civet standing in front of their college and giving them a big check for winning the Civet Prize, the check was SO big, and afterwards Lander gave a speech to the students and announced the next Civet Prize, which is to design the spacecraft that can best survive a simulated landing on Mars. The new prize is huge, it's a million dollars! I can't wait to tell Steve about it because he'll be really excited again now that there's a huge prize. Some people just need the extra motivation.

Oh yeah, I got an e-mail from Benji finally! It had some

pictures of him at a baseball game at Wrigley Field and him holding a fish they caught on Lake Michigan, and him and his mom and sister standing in front of a giant silver bean. That bean was SO huge. I wrote back to Benji and I told him the guys and me went to Las Vegas to find my dad but we lost Carl Sagan at Zelda's so we put up posters and called animal control, and then I met my Terra and saw her apartment which was a lot smaller than Paul Chung's apartment, and then we came to LA but we stopped at a lake because Terra really wanted to go swimming and we got here and Steve has so many Battlemorphs boosters, I'll see if I can get him one, and then we went to Ronnie's condo except he's in Detroit so we watched the sunset at Venice Beach and saw skateboarders and guys doing street gymnastics and then Steve and Terra had LOX and vodka and we were all dancing but not twerking, and we watched Contact except Terra fell asleep so we have to—

[door opening and closing]

ALEX: —finish watching it.

ALEX: Hey Steve!

ALEX: What's that behind your back?

STEVE: It's a surprise for Terra.

ALEX: Can I see?

STEVE: Sure, but keep it down.

ALEX (whispering): *They're daisies!*

STEVE: Do you think she'll like them?

ALEX: She'll love them. I'm suuuuure.

STEVE: Is she still sleeping?

ALEX: Nah, she's in Nathan's room and they're talking in private.

STEVE: They're talking . . .

ALEX: Yeah. They were just sitting on—

ALEX: Steve, make sure you knock first! They're having a private conversation!

[door opening]

TERRA (distant): *At least he—*

STEVE: *What . . .*

STEVE: *What the h—*

[muffled yelling]

TERRA: *Stop! . . . you're . . .*

[hurried footsteps]

ALEX: Guys? What are you . . .

TERRA: Oh god, he's bleed—

STEVE: Let GO of me—

TERRA: Stop! Just stop!

ALEX: Steve, stop! Why are you guys—

TERRA: Look what you're—

STEVE: Shut up! Shut u . . . y . . . [muffled]

ALEX: What . . .

STEVE: You heard me! Your sister is nothing but a—

TERRA: STOP IT.

[Alex crying]

TERRA: Look what you're doing. What is your *problem?*

STEVE: MY problem? I thought we were— I thought you— Why did it have to be Nath—

TERRA: We were just talking!

STEVE: Right, sure. You were just—

TERRA: We WERE!

STEVE: Stop lying to me! All I ever tried to do was be nice!

STEVE: I bought you flowers!

STEVE: I bought them for—HERE. Take your stupid daisies—

[Alex crying]

TERRA: *Alex . . .*

STEVE: Take this one, and this one, and—

TERRA: *Alex, are you OK?*

STEVE: —take all of them!

ALEX: *I want to go home.*

TERRA: *I'll take you home, Alex. We'll go—*

STEVE: That's right, take him home. Take him home to his deadbeat mom. That should've happened DAYS AGO. He shouldn't even BE HERE.

TERRA: Can't you see you're making him—

STEVE: I don't want anything to do with your dysfunctional—

TERRA: Alex, don't listen to him.

STEVE: No, listen to ME, Alex, because none of them are going to tell you the truth.

TERRA: Don't—

STEVE: You're never going to make a rocket that goes into space. It's impossible! You're a kid. A kid is never going to make a rocket that goes into—

TERRA: That's ENOUGH. Stop talking to him like—

STEVE: Like what? Like an adult? You want to lie to him and tell him everything's going to be OK, that he's going to do by himself what took thousands of people billions of dollars to do? And what do you think it'll solve Alex, HUH? You think it'll somehow bring your dad back or make your brother not want to—

TERRA: ENOUGH.

STEVE: —I have news for you, kid. You're going to wake up twenty years from now and your life is going to be a piece of—

TERRA: STEVE.

STEVE: —and the people who pretend to be your friends are going to stab you in the back—

TERRA: I wasn't— Nathan didn't—

STEVE: That's right, keep denying it. You think I'm an idiot, don't you? Well maybe I AM. Maybe it takes an IDIOT like me to tell Alex here how things work in the real world. An IDIOT who's not just going to feed him a bunch of false hopes!

STEVE: I'll tell you what, Alex, this IDIOT is going to do you a huge favor. He's going to throw your iPod out the—

[rustling]

[Alex crying]

TERRA: Don't you—

STEVE: Give me th—

NEW RECORDING 31
12M 49S

TERRA: —and an order of fries. Uh-huh.

TERRA: Alex, do you want anything else?

ALEX: Can we have fries à la mode?

TERRA: Do you have ice cream? Yeah. No.

TERRA: Are ice cream sandwiches OK?

ALEX: OK.

TERRA: Yeah, they're fine. Room 325. Thanks.

[hanging up phone]

ALEX: I wish you guys could have seen Terra. Steve was trying to take my Golden iPod and Terra was trying to stop him, and we were all pulling and pulling and then Terra punched him in the face.

TERRA: Yeah, well. He deserved it.

ALEX: I was really surprised you punched him. I think you gave him a black eye.

TERRA: I was surprised myself. And how we all just stood there, and he had that look on his face like—

TERRA: God, even thinking about it—

TERRA: He just makes me so mad.

ALEX: But it makes no sense. He brought you daisies! Why was he so mad and yelling at everyone and why would he try to hurt Nathan when you guys were just talking, and why did YOU hit HIM? Violence isn't the answer to anything.

TERRA: I thought Steve was going to hurt you too. I couldn't let him do that.

ALEX: So you hurt him before he could hurt me . . .

ALEX: I still don't understand why he was so mad though. I know he likes you . . . Did he think you liked Nathan? Was it because I told him you and Nathan were having a private—

TERRA: Hey. No. This has nothing to do with you, OK?

TERRA: Steve just thought . . .

ALEX: What?

ALEX: He thought what, Terra?

TERRA: Yes, he thought I liked Nathan. But it's more than that too. Sometimes people get into fights because they think . . . because they want the other person to be something that the other person isn't. Or doesn't want to be. They try to control people and when they find out they can't, they lose their sh—they can't handle it.

ALEX: But I thought he already had a girlfriend . . . Doesn't he love her?

TERRA: Steve doesn't understand what it means to be in love.

ALEX: What does it—

TERRA: I've met guys like him—they're not even real guys, they're just overgrown boys.

ALEX: I'm a boy.

TERRA: But at some point you'll become an adult, Alex. And when you do, you won't treat people the way Steve does. I know you won't.

TERRA: Forget about Steve. We're never seeing him again, OK?

ALEX: OK, but can you tell me what happened after Steve ran out of the apartment? I fell asleep. Tell them too.

TERRA: Alex, maybe you shouldn't record anything for a wh—

ALEX: Please?

TERRA: Alex—

ALEX: Please please please please pleaaase?

TERRA: All right.

TERRA: You did fall asleep, rocket scientist. You went to Zed's room to get away from all the drama and then you passed out. I don't blame you, I was exhausted from it too.

TERRA: I went in the bathroom and helped Nathan clean up some of the blood. Thank god his nose wasn't broken or anything, just swollen, and he had a small cut under his eye from his glasses.

TERRA: Then I packed up all our stuff and I told him I was taking you home to Rockview. I didn't want to be around when Steve got back.

ALEX: And that's when I woke up.

TERRA: That's when you woke up.

ALEX: And then we said good-bye to Nathan and I told him to tell Zed I'm sorry we couldn't stay and I hope he got lightened at his meditation seminar.

ALEX: What did Nathan say to you?

TERRA: Well, I told him I was sorry about the mess and he was just like, It happens. To be honest I was a little mad at him too, for not doing more. For not fighting back. But who knows, maybe Steve's pulled this kind of stuff before and Nathan's used to it.

ALEX: Terra, have you ever stayed in a hotel?

TERRA: I have, a few times.

ALEX: This one is so nice. The sheets are folded really good.

TERRA (laughing): I figured we could live it up for a night—we've still got a lot more road ahead of us.

ALEX: Can we see the Grand Canyon tomorrow?

TERRA: I wish we could, but we need to get you home.

Did you call your mom?

ALEX: I called her when you were in the shower and I told her we're coming back.

TERRA: What'd she say?

ALEX: She didn't say anything. I just left a message because she doesn't like to answer the phone when she's having one of her quiet days.

TERRA: Alex—

ALEX: You should call your mom too, Terra.

TERRA: And tell her what?

ALEX: Tell her you're taking me back to Rockview and you love her.

TERRA: I don't need another person yelling at me. I've had enough of that today.

ALEX: How do you know she's going to yell at you?

TERRA: I just know.

ALEX: Then I'll call her for you, and you can tell me what you want to say to her and I'll say it, and I'll tell you what she says back, and that way you won't have to hear her yelling at you.

TERRA: I wouldn't put you through that.

ALEX: Here, take your phone.

TERRA: ——

ALEX: Please?

TERRA: All right.

TERRA: Only because you asked.

ALEX (whispering): *OK guys, Terra's calling her mom.*

TERRA: Hey. It's me.

TERRA: Donna, I know—

ALEX: *Tell her you love her.*

TERRA: Mom—

TERRA: I love you.

TERRA: No, nothing's wrong—

TERRA: Why does there have to be something—

TERRA: Yeah. No.

TERRA: Sorry if I worried you.

TERRA: Yeah, he's still with me.

TERRA: I'm not in Vegas right now, that's why I wasn't there.

TERRA: You don't want to know. I'm taking him home to Colorado.

TERRA: It's hard for me to explain right now.

TERRA: They don't seem—

TERRA: He doesn't really have anyone else.

TERRA: I know, I'll be careful, Mom. I know.

TERRA: I'm not sure when.

TERRA: Uh-huh. Tell Howard I said hi.

TERRA: You too. Bye.

[sniffling]

ALEX: Did she yell at you?

TERRA: Come here. Give me a hug.

[rustling]

ALEX: Terra?

TERRA: Hmm.

ALEX: Is it true what Steve said?

TERRA: About what?

ALEX: That it's impossible for me to launch a rocket into space.

TERRA: Steve's a jerk. Don't let anyone tell you something's impossible.

ALEX: But if it's the truth like he said, I want to know. Is it?

TERRA: It's . . . very tough.

ALEX: But is it impossible?

TERRA: It's not impossible. But it's probably more than one person can handle on their own. All those rocket scientists had a lot of help, and it took them a crazy amount of work and time. Maybe longer than you can imagine right now.

ALEX: I can imagine a lot.

TERRA: I know you can. And if there's anyone who can launch that rocket, I think it's you, Alex. Not a lot of people have what you have.

ALEX: What do I have?

TERRA: You have a plan, a mission. You know what you want. Most people give up on what they want. They'll come across the first little obstacle and they'll give up, and then they'll try to tear down the people they see doing what they felt like they couldn't. That's what Steve was trying to do. It was about him, not me or you.

ALEX: I have something else too now.

TERRA: What is it?

ALEX: I have a Terra. And you're going to be my lot of help, you're going to help me find all the sounds from Earth and we're going to redouble our efforts and build Voyager 4 together, and next year we'll go to SHARF again to launch it.

TERRA: Alex . . .

ALEX: It's weird though, because I keep thinking about what the older kid said—

TERRA: The older kid?

ALEX: The one who pretended to be my adult and helped me get on the train but then he got sick, remember? I thought you listened to my recordings!

TERRA: OK, the older kid, yeah. Remind me what he said.

ALEX: He said he hopes I find what I'm looking for. And I hoped so too, but what's weird is that I was looking for sounds from Earth and a man in love and then I found out I had a maybe dad, and then I was looking for my maybe dad but I found my Terra instead, and I'm glad I found you, I'm SO glad, but I still don't really have a dad and I don't have a man in love either because I don't think it's Steve, and it's like, I'm never finding what I'm looking for, I'm always finding something else, and there are other things I'm looking for too now, like Carl Sagan, so am I not going to find him either?

TERRA: That's not true—

ALEX: Then what is?

ALEX: What is, Terra?

[knocking on door]

UNIDENTIFIED MALE: *Room service.*

TERRA: That's our food . . .

ALEX: Terra?

ALEX: Tell me, are we going to find him?

ALEX: What's the truth?

[knocking on door]

TERRA: I don't know.

ALEX: You don't know?

TERRA: The truth is I don't know.

ALEX: But there's a chance, right? It's not impossible.

TERRA: There's definitely a chance.

[knocking on door]

TERRA: There's always a chance.

UNIDENTIFIED MALE: *Room service.*

NEW RECORDING 32
3M 29S

Hi guys, I called Ronnie again this morning when we left the hotel. I told him, Me and Terra are on our way back to Rockview and how's it going with your prospective client? And he said, What! I told you to stay in LA! and he was shouting and there was a lot of noise in the background, I think he was at his basketball showcase. I told him again that me and Terra are going back to Rockview except I shouted it so he could hear me, and he said, Fine! Even better! Call me when you get home!

We've been driving for six hours already but we weren't driving for all those six hours, we stopped at gas stations and for lunch. We're at a gas station right now. Terra really wanted to get to Rockview tonight but she said she doesn't think she can drive for another six hours, so how about let's try to reach Santa Fe before dark and find a motel? I said, Why don't we sleep in the car or find a place to go camping because I don't want my Terra to waste all her money, and she said camping is a great idea.

I started looking on Google Maps for camping places and it said we're going to drive near Taos, New Mexico, and I remembered that Ken Russell's store is Taos, New Mexico!

I showed Terra the business card Ken gave me at SHARF and she said we should call him, maybe he'll let us crash, and I said, But if we crash then how are we going to get to Rockview without fixing the car? Terra laughed and said it's not that kind of crashing, it's the other kind, like when you're at a friend's house and it's late and you're too tired to drive home so you spend the night. I said, Oh, you mean like a sleepover, and Terra said that's exactly it, we'll call Ken and ask him if we can have a sleepover in his yard.

I called Ken Russell and I said, Hey Ken, it's me, we met at SHARF and I helped you set up the launchurdles and I tried to launch Voyager 3 but it failed and you gave me a T-shirt for Best First Effort, and then I went to Las Vegas with Steve and Zed and my pup Carl Sagan who you met also, but we lost him at Zelda's and we looked for him and put up posters and called animal control but they haven't seen him, and then we went to my maybe dad's address and I met my Terra and we went to LA with the guys but Ronnie wasn't home, and we had a dance party and Steve broke Nathan's glasses and made his nose bleed and he tried to take my iPod so Terra gave him a black eye and now she's taking me back to Rockview and last night we stayed in a hotel and now we're on I-40 and we'll be in Taos, New Mexico, in two and a half hours and can we crash at your house but the sleepover kind of crash, not the accident kind.

Ken didn't say anything for a long time and I thought maybe Terra's phone had no signal or the call failed so I said, Hello? and Ken said, Who is this again? so at least we didn't get disconnected. I started telling him again but Terra said to give her the phone, and I told her I don't want us to accident crash, and she said just put it on speakerphone then. She talked to Ken and explained again about me meeting him at SHARF, and then she asked him can we camp in his yard because we already have my tent and we'll be gone in the morning. Ken said he's going to check with his wife and he'll call us back, and then we stopped for—

[phone ringing]

That's Ken right now! Hold on guys, I have to take this.

NEW RECORDING 33
2M 21S

Ken Russell's house is on a gravel road, and when we got here I said, Hey Ken, your street is so bumpy, I think you need a civil engineer. I almost didn't recognize Ken at first because his bushy beard was shaved, and now he just has a bushy mustache that curls up on both sides toward the end. It's still pretty majestic though.

Ken told us to come in but keep our voices down because his baby daughter Hannah is taking a nap, and he said Mrs. Russell, whose first name is Diane, isn't home yet, she's visiting a patient. Mrs. Russell is a physical therapist. I asked Ken, What's the difference between a physical therapist and a regular therapist, because my mom used to go to a therapist when I was in second grade but then she stopped going because Ronnie said it was a waste of money. Ken said that Mrs. Russell works with people with disabilities or who've been in accidents and have problems with their back, and she helps them learn how to move again. I told him that when we were driving Terra said her back was sore so maybe she should make an appointment.

Ken said let's go out to the observatory and that way we can talk in our normal voices, and I said, You have an observatory! and then I covered my mouth because I didn't mean to say it so loud. I was too excited. We went through part of the backyard which is huge and most of it is yellow dirt and little brown bushes and there's no fence between his yard and his neighbors' yards, it's perfect for launching rockets.

I found out Ken's observatory isn't a real observatory though, Ken just calls it that because there's an upstairs part with glass windows all the way around and the downstairs is Mrs. Russell's office. But it's still pretty cool. It has Ken's telescope and a rug and floor pillows, and a coffee table with science and yoga magazines on it along with some of Hannah's toys. There was a model of a Saturn V rocket in a glass case too but that was the only one, and I said, Hey Ken, where's all your other rocket stuff? He said he just keeps it at his store.

After we saw the sort-of observatory Ken invited us to join them for dinner, he said he's making pizza and salad. Mrs. Russell got home and she kissed Ken and said hello to us, and then she changed into gym clothes and went for a run and Terra went with her even though Terra didn't have running shoes, she just had her sneakers.

Now Ken's chopping vegetables in the kitchen and I'm helping watch Hannah because she just woke up from her nap, and she reminds me of Benji's sister except she doesn't like walking, she likes wiggling instead. She's like a giant worm. I tried to hold her and show her how to play with her toys but she just kept wiggling away and her shoe kept falling off. Every time I put it back on it fell off again! And then she started almost crying but I didn't know why she was almost crying, and I was trying to make her feel better so I started saying the launch sequence because sometimes that makes me feel better. I would say five . . . four . . . three . . . and her eyes would get really big and I would say two . . . one . . . and her eyes would still be really big and she'd shake her arms like she wanted me to hurry up, and then I would go *pwooooosh* and then she'd laugh. I don't think she liked the counting, she just liked the pwooshes. I told her she has to learn patience.

Hannah's watching me talk to you guys now and her eyes are really big again, and—

[Hannah shrieking]

Um, I think she wants the iPod.

[Hannah speaking gibberish]

Maybe she wants to record something for you g—

Hey . . . stop! I'm ticklish!

[Alex laughing]

Hey Ken, I think we got a future astronomer on our hands!

[Ken laughing]

[Hannah speaking gibberish]

NEW RECORDING 34
14M 50S

ALEX: —are you sure? I can record somewhere else if you want to—

ALEX: Oops, it already started.

TERRA: It's all right, I don't think I'm falling asleep any time soon.

ALEX: But I thought you were tired from driving.

TERRA: I guess not.

TERRA: Don't let me stop you. Besides, I like watching you make your recordings.

ALEX: OK. I'll try not to talk too loud just in case you want to sleep.

ALEX: Hi guys, you probably think me and Terra are camping in the Russells' yard but we're not, we're in the observatory. Ken and Mrs. Russell told us we can sleep here, we don't have to sleep outside, and also they got out their Aerobed which is a kind of air mattress! It's so much better than sleeping on hard ground.

The pizza that Ken made for dinner was so good, by the way. He gave me the recipe and I'm going to try making it for my mom when I get home. At dinner me and Terra told him and Mrs. Russell about everything that happened after SHARF and how we figured out we have the same dad, and Ken said it seems a lot's happened in my life since we last saw each other. I told him it seems like a lot's happened with his beard, too.

Mrs. Russell said thank goodness that I'm on my way back home now. She said whenever she's away from home for more than a couple days she starts to get homesick, and she said also that when she was a little girl she accidentally left their front door open and HER dog ran away too. But then one of their neighbors found him and brought him back, and she hopes that Carl Sagan turns up.

After dinner Mrs. Russell put Hannah to bed while the rest of us cleaned up the table and washed the dishes, and Ken and I told Terra about how everyone on Rocketforum is really excited about this weekend's Mars launch. We talked about my hero too, and Ken told me he first saw the original *Cosmos* TV show when he was in college and he even recorded every episode on VHS tapes. I asked him what are VHS tapes and what does VHS stand for, and he said it's Video Home something, he's not really sure. He said they're kind of like Blu-rays except they're big and clunky and use magnetic tape instead of a disc, and the tapes would always get jammed because of all the moving parts and the whole thing was really inelegant. I said, Oh, you mean they're like the ancestor of all the mammals which looked something like a shrew but it's still a really important step in our evolution, so maybe VHS was like the shrew of watching shows in your house. Ken said it's a great metaphor.

After that we came out to the observatory to look through Ken's telescope but it was cloudy so we couldn't see much, and then Terra was going to get our tent from her car but that's when Mrs. Russell said we don't have to sleep outside, we can sleep in the observatory. Her and Ken got us the Aerobed and pillows and blankets also, and they brought us water too because they're really good hosts.

TERRA: I agree one hundred percent. And there's something amazing about their chemistry together.

ALEX: Their chem—

TERRA: It's like . . . the way when two people are together, they can make something more. Like, a third thing.

ALEX: You mean Hannah?

TERRA (laughing): That too, but I'm talking more about a kind of energy that two people have. It's like . . . something you can almost see, and feel, that's clear to anyone who's there with them. Like, even from the way they talk to each other—you can hear it in their voices.

ALEX: You can tell they're in love.

TERRA: Exactly.

ALEX: Maybe they fell in love like my mom and our dad, and like your mom and our dad.

TERRA: Maybe . . .

ALEX: OH! Maybe Ken could be my man in love!

TERRA: Hmm . . .

ALEX: I'll ask him in the morning.

TERRA: You know, Diane told me—when we were out running before dinner—she told me that after she and Ken got engaged they actually lived apart for a while. His mom was sick so he was moving back to be near her, but things were just starting to pick up with Diane's physical therapy practice in San Francisco and she wanted to stay.

ALEX: But she's here now . . . Did she change her mind?

TERRA: That's what I asked, and she said it wasn't that her mind changed, really, but more that she had to stay until *she* was ready. And Ken had to go, and he was mad that she didn't want to come with him, and she was mad at him for wanting her to give up her life in San

Francisco. They'd fight about it all the time, she said.

ALEX: But don't they love each other? If they're in love why would they fight . . .

TERRA: It's—it's complicated. Just because you love someone doesn't mean you never get into fights. But when you really love each other, you can work through it, usually.

ALEX: Terra?

TERRA: Hmm?

ALEX: Have you ever been in love?

TERRA: I have, once.

ALEX: Was it your fling?

TERRA: No, this was different. It was real.

ALEX: But . . . I don't get it, what's the difference between real love and not-real love? How do you know that time was real? How can you tell?

TERRA: It's something that you can feel deep inside. It's like, when you feel it, you just know. It's hard to describe.

ALEX: Is it wanting to French-kiss somebody?

TERRA: Sometimes it involves that, but it's much more than that too. There's a part of it that's, like, letting go. Like a sacrifice but in a good way. You trade a part of yourself for something that's even bigger than you, and it feels good but weird at the same time. It's totally worth it, though.

ALEX: But how do you know? There has to be a way you can know. Can't you measure their heartbeats and brainwaves like my hero did? Can't you tell from those? And also you JUST said you can tell Ken and Mrs. Russell are in love, so how do you know?

TERRA: Mmm . . . maybe you can't *really* know, from the outside. Maybe only the people who are in it can really know.

ALEX: Then, how can we tell if our dad loved my mom? Or if he loved your mom?

TERRA: I . . .

ALEX: Or were they just flings.

TERRA: They weren't flings. I don't know. I don't remember much more about him than you do.

ALEX: What do you remember?

TERRA: I remember . . . I remember he'd pick me up and rub his chin against the side of my face, and I'd squirm and try to get away because his stubble tickled my cheek.

TERRA: It's weird, I have mostly these random sense memories of him. I mean, it's not like I saw him that often. I knew he lived somewhere else even though I didn't exactly know where. He'd stop by whenever he was in town. Donna would be dating other men, but he'd still come by the house to see me.

TERRA: One time he bought me a baseball glove and

Donna was *not* happy about that. She didn't want me to get too used to the idea of him being around, I guess. But I loved that thing. We'd play catch and he would throw the ball really hard—he didn't hold back because I was a girl. That's what I remember—the way the ball stung when it smacked the inside of the glove, the way my palm would go numb.

TERRA: But then . . . he had this whole other life that I didn't know about. With you and your mom and Ronnie. I mean, I kind of knew that he had another family but I didn't really ask. I guess I didn't really want to know . . .

ALEX: Well, now you know some of it, and tomorrow you're going to meet my mom and you'll know more, and then I'll show you my house and my room and all my stuff, like my hero's books and my tesseract and my—

TERRA: Your tesseract?

TERRA: You mean like in those superhero movies?

ALEX: Oh, no, that's different. A tesseract is a four-dimensional object. My science teacher Mr. Fogerty gave it to me.

TERRA: But, I mean, what does it look like?

ALEX: It looks like a clear cube inside another cube.

TERRA: I still don't . . .

ALEX: OK, you know how a square has two dimensions and a cube has three dimensions, right?

TERRA: Right.

ALEX: A tesseract is the four-dimensional version of a cube.

TERRA: OK . . .

ALEX: But actually what I have isn't a REAL tesseract, it's just a shadow of a tesseract. It's a shadowract.

TERRA: A shadow . . .

ALEX: Yeah, because cubes have shadows that are flat, so tesseracts have shadows that are three-dimensional, and because WE'RE three-dimensional, that's the only way we can kind of see tesseracts—through their shadows.

TERRA: Oh.

ALEX: It's probably easier if I just show you when we get to my house.

TERRA: OK . . .

ALEX: Are you still confused?

TERRA: What? Oh—no, it's not . . . I mean, yeah.

TERRA: But I also just have a lot on my mind.

ALEX: Like what?

ALEX: Terra?

TERRA: Like, I've been getting voicemails from my manager at the restaurant, asking why I haven't been in. Amy's been texting me too. She can't cover for me forever. I mean, maybe I shouldn't meet your mom tomorrow. Maybe I should just drop you off in Rockview and go back to Vegas.

ALEX: But . . . why?

TERRA: I don't know. I don't know what's going to happen if I meet your mom. I'm worried the universe might explode.

ALEX: I don't think that's possible though.

TERRA: You don't?

ALEX: Because the universe already exploded 13.8 billion years ago. It's still exploding right now, kind of.

TERRA: Alex . . .

TERRA: Hey, tell me some astronomy jokes. Maybe they'll calm my nerves.

ALEX: Um . . . have you heard the joke about the astronomer and the observatory?

TERRA: I haven't.

ALEX: It's a long joke.

TERRA: We have time.

ALEX: OK.

ALEX: There were two astronomers, Henry and Nick, and they were the bestest of friends. They both worked at an observatory at the end of a mountain road where there used to be a potato farm.

ALEX: One weekend Nick was coming back from a trip but his flight got delayed, so when he finally landed Monday night he had to go straight into work. He was so tired that he fell asleep at his desk, and he dreamed about the most beautiful meteor shower he had ever seen.

TERRA: How beautiful was it?

ALEX: It was SO beautiful. They should've sent a poet.

TERRA: Beautiful. Keep going.

ALEX: So Nick dreamed about the beautiful meteor shower but then a loud BOOM woke him up. He looked around and the instruments were still working, but no one was there. He said, Henry! Where are you guys? but nobody answered, and then he heard another BOOM, and then the sound of falling rocks, and he remembered something about a meteor shower that he was watching or supposed to be watching.

He headed for the observatory door, and when he got outside he heard the boom again, even louder this time—BOOM!—and he even saw a bright orange streak from the corner of his eye. But as soon as he turned to look, it was gone.

Nick started running down the mountain path. There was another boom, and then more rocks, and he ran toward the sounds. Nick could see Henry now, him and some of the other astronomers were standing with flashlights at the end of a big empty field. He ran up to them and yelled, Henry! Henry! Where did the meteor land?

And when Nick got there, Henry was holding a long cannon made from white plumbing pipes. There was one more loud BOOOOM, the loudest yet, and the cannon shot out a flaming potato that sailed across the sky.

And Henry said to him, That's not a meteor, it's a *spud*, Nick!

[crickets]

[Terra giggling]

[Alex giggling]

[both laughing]

ALEX: It's funny because it sounds like the Russian satellite *Sputnik*.

NEW RECORDING 35
6M 51S

Guys you won't believe what happened! You won't believe— Oops.

Sorry. Terra is still asleep. I'll try to be quiet.

We left Taos pretty early this morning but before we left, Ken said he has a gift for me, and he gave me a box and inside the box was an old telescope! He said he found it when he was looking for his *Cosmos* VHS tapes earlier and since he already has a telescope I can have this one!

But that's not the thing you guys won't believe happened.

We said good-bye to the Russells—

Oh no! I just realized I forgot to ask Ken to be my man in love! I can't believe I forgot . . . Maybe we can . . . No, it's too far.

Sorry guys, I'll remember to call him and ask. We can do it over the phone probably. That should still work.

Anyway, we said good-bye to the Russells and got on the highway, and there were big rain curtains in the distance and lightning too, and after a while the highway curved and we were driving right into the storm. It was raining so hard, it was tough to see the road even though Terra turned on the headlights and put the windshield wipers to the fastest setting. I said, Hey Terra, I think this is a monsoon so maybe we should pull over, but Terra said let's keep going, we're already in it now and maybe the best way out is just to go through.

I really didn't want us to accident crash but I also wanted to get to Rockview ASAP so Terra could meet my mom, and I guess Terra did too.

So we kept driving and whenever we passed a semi-truck its wheels would splash a ton of water on us and Terra would go faster to get out of its wake, and we didn't stop at any restaurants or gas stations but we had some snacks that Mrs. Russell gave us, so we ate those for our lunch. It seemed like the storm was going to go on forever but then the rain got lighter all of a sudden, and then Terra put her windshield wipers back to the slowest setting. I thought that maybe we were in the eye of the monsoon but I wasn't sure if monsoons have eyes like hurricanes, but I guess not because the rain stayed light after that. Then I fell asleep and I woke up exactly when we turned onto my street, it was so weird. It was like I was the radio telescopes at the Very Large Array in *Contact* and it's all static and then there's a signal and it starts going *vwooaww vwooaww vwooaww vwooaww* except instead of detecting extra-terrestrial intelligence it was me detecting when I was close to my house.

The drive took us six hours even though it should've taken us four hours. When we got to my house finally, it was still raining a little but it wasn't monsooning, and I took out my keys from my duffel bag and opened the door, and everything was so quiet because Carl Sagan wasn't there to wag his tail and jump on me. Terra asked me what's wrong and I said, How can I keep forgetting about my best friend? and Terra said what about my mom, and I told Terra that my mom's one of my best friends too, but I'm referring to Carl Sagan. Terra asked me is my mom home and I said, Oh, let me check!

We went to the door of her bedroom and knocked on it and I said, Mom? Are you home? And there was no answer, so I opened it and she wasn't there. I told Terra, My mom's probably on one of her walks and I hope she brought an umbrella. Terra asked me when will she be back and I said, It depends on if she turned left or right at Justin Mendoza's house but we can go up to the roof to look for her if you want. Then I saw Terra yawn again like she was doing in the car and I told her she should take a nap and meet my mom later when she comes back. Terra said OK.

I showed Terra my room and she laid down in Ronnie's bed, and I got my tesseract from my shelf to show her but by the time I turned around she was already asleep, she didn't even take off her shoes! So I took off her shoes for her and then I went to the closet in the hallway and got her a blanket because she was lying on the one that was already on the bed.

When I came out I was going to call animal control again but I saw the flashing light on our voicemail which means there are new messages, so I listened to the messages. A few of them were the ones I left for my mom when I was in New Mexico and Las Vegas and LA. There was a message Ronnie left for our mom too, and a message from someone named Juanita from the Colorado Department of Human Services asking my mom to call her. And the very LAST voicemail was from a nice lady from Las Vegas named Janine Maplethorn and SHE SAID SHE FOUND CARL SAGAN! SHE FOUND— Oops.

I'm being too loud again.

In her message Janine Maplethorn said she saw my name and phone number on Carl Sagan's collar and what a strange name for a dog. I called her back right away but it was hard to talk at first, it was like there was a big water balloon inside my chest and when Janine Maplethorn said, Hello? it was like someone pricked the balloon and all the water came out and flooded my insides, and I tried to talk but I couldn't, and it was a little hard to breathe too, and I thought maybe that's how Zed felt when he was doing his vow of silence.

But then I could finally talk again, and I told Janine Maplethorn that I got her message about Carl Sagan and I asked her can I talk to him and where did she find him? And she said she found him hiding under her car when she was leaving the nail salon. She put him on and I said, Hi, boy! It's me, Alex! and I think he recognized my voice because I could hear his collar jingling.

Janine Maplethorn asked me how old am I, and I told her I'm eleven but at least thirteen in responsibility years, and she said, You need to take care of your dog, kid, he's a long way from home. And I said, Yeah he is, he ran out when I was in Las Vegas with the guys after we were all at SHARF and my rocket failed, and then I met my Terra and we went to LA to see Ronnie, and then Janine Maplethorn said, Well why don't you get in that rocket of yours and come pick up your dog?

I told her I can't do that because for a rocket that size it's really expensive right now, that's why Lander Civet is working on reusable rockets. Janine Maplethorn said in that case tell my friends in Vegas or LA or wherever to come get Carl Sagan because she ain't gonna take care of him forever, and I said, That's a great idea—when Terra wakes up from her nap I'll tell her to ask her mom because her mom lives in Las Vegas. Janine Maplethorn gave me the address and she said, Tell her to hurry her bleep over because your dog won't stop farting!

And I said that's because you need to feed him natural turkey-based gluten- and dairy-free kibble, he has a sensitive digestive system.

NEW RECORDING 36
2H 4M 14S

[pan sizzling]

Hi guys, can you hear me?

If it's a little noisy that's because I'm cooking dinner right now so hopefully you can hear me.

My mom's not home yet, she's still on her walk, but I bet she'll be really happy when she gets back and sees that I'm making food for us again. She finished all the stuff in the refrigerator and she made some of her own food too, and I could tell because all the dirty plates and pans and empty GladWares were in the sink when we got here. I went up to the roof earlier to see if I could see her but I couldn't, and then I left Terra a note telling her I'm going to Safeway to get groceries.

But then I didn't even need the note because Terra was still sleeping when I got back! She must've been really exhausted.

[spatula scraping]

I wish I could record smells onto this Golden iPod for you guys. For the Golden Record my hero converted pictures into binary, which is ones and zeros, so maybe I can come up with a way to convert smells to binary because I don't think that technology exists yet. If it did, I'd record the smell of spinach which I'm cooking right now and the smell of mashed potatoes with sour cream and butter, which I already made. I'd record the smell of baked pork chops too, which are my mom's favorite. She loves pork chops so much. One time she went to Safeway and she bought seven pounds of pork chops and she came back and ate all seven pounds of it in one sitting and she didn't even cook it, that's how much she loves pork chops.

[spatula scraping]

There, all done.

[drawer opening]

[utensils clanking]

I'm going to go see if Terra's awake yet.

[footsteps]

[knocking on door]

ALEX: Hey Terra?

[door creaking]

ALEX: Are you awake yet?

TERRA: Mmm.

ALEX: Terra, you've been asleep for four and a half hours.

TERRA: That long?

ALEX: That long.

ALEX: Dinner's almost ready, I made baked pork chops and spinach and mashed potatoes and I have great news! Janine Maplethorn found Carl Sagan!

TERRA: That's great! Who's Janine Maplethorn?

ALEX: She's a nice lady in Las Vegas. She called and left a message and I called her back. Can you call your mom and tell her to pick up Carl Sagan and hurry her bleep over there?

TERRA (laughing): Of course.

TERRA: Your mom—is she back yet?

ALEX: She's not back yet.

TERRA: Alex, is she . . .

ALEX: Terra?

TERRA: Hmm?

ALEX: Your breath stinks.

TERRA (laughing): Great.

ALEX: You can use my mouthwash, it's the blue-green bottle in the medicine cabinet in the bathroom. And I put a new toothbrush in the toothbrush holder for you, it's the one with the red handle.

TERRA: Rocket scientist, you're a sweetheart. You're going to make Dr. Judith Bloomington a happy lady someday.

TERRA: Just give me a few minutes, OK? I'll come out in a bit.

ALEX: OK! I'll go look for my mom again!

[hurried footsteps]

[garage door opening]

[rustling]

[door closing]

[toilet flushing]

[door opening]

[drawers opening and closing]

TERRA: Where do they keep the . . .

TERRA: Oh, this must be that thing he was talking about. A cube inside a cube.

TERRA: And he forgot his . . .

TERRA: Hey, Alex?

TERRA: Where'd you go!

ALEX (distant): *I'm out here!*

TERRA: Alex, do you guys have any aspirin!

TERRA: And you left your iPod on the bed!

ALEX: *It's in the—*

ALEX: *Whoaa—*

[loud crash]

TERRA: Alex?

[Alex screaming]

TERRA: Alex!

[hurried footsteps]

[Alex screaming louder]

TERRA (distant): *Alex!*

[dogs barking]

TERRA: *Don't move, OK? I'm going to—*

[Alex screaming]

TERRA: *Hello! Hello! Help! My brother he . . .* [muffled]

TERRA: *No he's—*

[Alex screaming]

[dogs barking]

TERRA: Keys keys where are the—

TERRA: Keys!

[door slamming]

TERRA: *Hold on!*

[Alex screaming]

[dogs barking]

[car doors slamming]

[engine starting]

[tires squealing]

[engine accelerating]

[dogs barking]

[doorbell ringing]

UNIDENTIFIED MALE: *Hello?*

[doorbell ringing]
UNIDENTIFIED MALE: *Is anyone home?*
[knocking on door]

UNIDENTIFIED MALE: *We heard yelling from down the street, is everything OK?*
[knocking on door]
UNIDENTIFIED MALE: *Hello?*

[cars passing]

[birds chirping]

[car passing]

[crickets]

[car passing]

[crickets]

NEW RECORDING 37
3M 15S

It's Terra. Alex is in the Recovery Ward. He came out of surgery an hour ago. Or was it two hours? I don't even know. I called his house, his brother, I called my mom and Howard, I called everyone. It's three in the morning, they're all asleep.

God I hate hospitals. I'm not allowed to see him yet. The nurse said they're not sure how long he'll be in Recovery before they can move him. And it wasn't doing me any good just waiting there, I was totally use-less. I couldn't fill out any of his paperwork—I didn't have his insurance, I didn't even know his mom's first name!

I came back to the house to try to find her. When I drove up her car was in the garage and I thought she was finally home, but then I remembered it'd been there when we'd first arrived, too. There was a huge dent in the fender—I hadn't noticed that before. Didn't Alex say that she doesn't drive anymore? Something is very, very wrong here. I looked in her room again and the bed was made—was it like that earlier? Or did Alex do that . . . and there were stacks of those newspaper things, what do you call them—coupon flyers—all along the wall. Like towers. Covered in dust. It was like nobody lived there at all. And I've been thinking, What if she hasn't been around for a while now? What if she hasn't been around for more than just a while? Oh god, I mean, what if Alex made her up? Like, he's been pretending she's still around and—and just couldn't come to terms with her not being here anymore? Come to think of it, I've never heard him talk directly to her on the phone . . . No, that can't be right. Can it? How is it possible, how could he live in this house all by himself? What is going on?

Karen. That's her name. His mom's name is Karen.

Why am I even talking into this thing. I have no idea. On our way to the hospital Alex kept mumbling for his iPod, saying it's still recording, the battery's going to run out. I kept telling him I'll get it, I'll bring it to you. Maybe I should've waited for an ambulance but before I knew what I was doing we were already in my car. I don't even remember looking up directions. Just now I went outside to where Alex fell and the lawn, it's all overgrown. It's like nobody's mowed it in years. And the ladder was still tipped over on the fence and there was blood on the end of that stick or whatever that was. A piece of the fence. At least it didn't go in too deep, maybe an inch—oh god. Maybe I shouldn't have pulled it out. I should've left it in. I mean, why was he trying to go up to the roof with that telescope?

I'm still here now—at the house. I threw away that stick and put everything else back in the garage, and when I came back in I saw the dinner that Alex had made for us. It was still on the table, completely untouched, and I realized that I hadn't eaten anything since we were driving from the Russells'. I didn't even use a fork. And then I tried putting the leftovers in the fridge but I was having trouble doing the simplest things, it took me ten minutes to find a Tupperware the right size. I tried calling Ronnie again and stopped and started like five times. Should I go back to the hospital? Should I stay here and wait for his mom? I tried listening to his recordings from before the accident but I couldn't listen to more than a few seconds. Just hearing his voice—I kept seeing him hanging over that fence and . . .

NEW RECORDING 38
3M 26S

It's me again.

They still haven't moved Alex to a regular room yet.

I don't know what's taking so long.

They haven't given me any real reasons either, other than they need to keep an eye on his condition. It's just been a lot of waiting around.

Nothing but waiting.

I did finally get ahold of Ronnie. I told him what happened and he was weirdly quiet, at least at first. He was probably just in shock. I asked him if their mom was still around and living in their house, and he was like, What do you mean, of course she's around. I told him about the dusty room and the coupon flyers and he said he'd try to figure out what's going on. Then I asked him when he's flying in and he said, But Alex is going to be

OK, right? They're going to move him to a room and then he'll just need to rest for a while?

And that's when it occurred to me that he doesn't want to come, he doesn't want—

Ha! I can't even get mad anymore. I'm too exhausted.

Anyway I blew up at him, and he started yelling back at me, asking me what good would it do, what does it matter if he comes today or in a couple days, Alex will still be in the hospital. I was like, What's wrong with you, Alex needs to be with family, and then Ronnie goes off on me like, who am I to know what's best for his family. But after all that, he told me to stay put, he'll take the next flight out. I guess he finally came to his senses.

I tried listening to Alex's recordings again. I made it a little further this time, but then I got to that one recording—of the night we got to the guys' place. When we were drinking and dancing . . .

How could I have been so . . . so . . .

I felt sick, listening to that recording. Knowing I'd acted like that. Around *him*. That I . . .

[muffled crying]

And then I got to the part where . . . and I couldn't . . . I couldn't listen anymore. And I couldn't stay . . . the waiting room. I had to . . .

[sniffling]

I got in my car and started driving. Just driving around, not going anywhere.

There aren't that many streetlamps in this town . . . Or they turn them off at night or something. The traffic lights were all flashing yellow, and it was actually comforting, in a way. To be moving. To be two headlights going down the street, while everyone and everything else is sleeping.

I passed a gas station that was still open and I turned around. I went in and bought a pack of gum. I tried to peel off the plastic but my hands were shaking, they were shaking so badly, but I finally managed to get it open, and the attendant was like, Are you OK? and I was like, No.

And now I'm just standing outside, in front of the building. Just staring at the gas pumps. I've been here for I don't know how long . . .

I mean, what am I even *doing*?

What am I *supposed* to do?

Can you at least tell me that?

No, of course you can't, because I'm asking for answers from a freaking iPod.

NEW RECORDING 39
4M 10S

TERRA: It's on.

TERRA: Do you want to hold it?

ALEX: ——

TERRA: I'm going to put it right here by your hand, OK?

ALEX: ——

TERRA: Do you want some water, or apple juice?

ALEX: ——

TERRA: All right, if you want it just let me know.

ALEX: ——

TERRA: Alex, I want you to listen closely and I want you to be totally honest with me. You know that you can tell me anything, right?

ALEX: ——

TERRA: Nod if you understand me.

ALEX: ——

TERRA: You said your mom went on one of her walks.

TERRA: Do you know where she goes? On these walks.

ALEX: ——

TERRA: Have you ever gone with her?

[Alex groaning]

TERRA: Here, I'll get it.

[hospital bed inclining]

TERRA: Go ahead, sip.

[straw croaking]

TERRA: Do you want more? I can ask the nurse to bring more.

ALEX: ——

TERRA: OK, just let me know if you do.

TERRA: Alex, when your mom goes on her walks—how long is she usually gone?

TERRA: An hour?

ALEX: ——

TERRA: No?

[Alex groaning]

TERRA: Don't try to talk, just hold up your fingers.

TERRA: Three? Three hours? And then she comes back?

ALEX: ——

TERRA: Has she ever not come back?

[Alex groaning]

TERRA: Alex, I know it's hard right now. Hang in there a little longer and help me understand.

TERRA: I just want to know the truth. Your hero believed in the truth, right?

ALEX: ——

TERRA: Good. Now tell me—has your mom ever not come back after a few hours?

ALEX: ——

TERRA: What's the longest she's been gone?

ALEX: ——

TERRA: How long, Alex. Show me with your fingers.

ALEX: ——

TERRA: Hours?

ALEX: ——

TERRA: No? So, DAYS? OK, days . . .

TERRA: Alex, I have to go make a call, OK? I'll be right outside.

ALEX: ——

[curtain opening]

[curtain closing]

TERRA (distant): *I need to report a missing—*

[hospital bed inclining]

[hospital bed reclining]

[hospital bed inclining]

[hospital bed reclining]

[hospital bed inclining]

[hospital bed reclining]

[curtain opening]

[Alex groaning]

TERRA: What is it?

TERRA: Don't you want your iPod?

ALEX: ——

TERRA: All right, I'll hold on to it. You just focus on getting better.

TERRA: You can have it back when you're better, OK?

ALEX: ——

TERRA: That's my rocket scientist.

TERRA: Now get some rest.

NEW RECORDING 40
10M 48S

TERRA: Alex, look.

TERRA: Someone came to see you.

ALEX: Oh, hi Steve.

TERRA (to Steve): He's still a little out of it.

STEVE: I brought you something.

ALEX: What is it?

TERRA: See for yourself.

[bag crinkling]

ALEX: Johnny Rockets!

TERRA: Too bad he can't eat any right now.

ALEX: That's right. I'm on a liquid diet.

STEVE: Sorry, I should've asked first.

ALEX: It smells so good though. I wish I could eat it by smelling it. But then I'd be on a gas diet.

TERRA: But he's still very much himself, as you can see.

TERRA: Hey Alex, let's go over by the window. Steve brought another surprise for you too.

ALEX: He did?

TERRA: Go take a look.

[hospital bed inclining]

TERRA: Careful now.

TERRA (to Steve): He was having trouble walking earlier.

ALEX: Uh-huh. I was so dizzy. But Dr. Clemens said I have to keep moving because, um, I forgot . . .

TERRA: Something about not letting his organs stick to his spine.

TERRA: OK, right down there. See him?

ALEX: CARL SAGAN! And Zed! You brought him thank you thank—oww . . .

TERRA: Careful—

STEVE: Are you OK?

ALEX: It still hurts sometimes.

STEVE: Sorry, I tried to bring Carl Sagan inside but they only allow service animals.

TERRA: Steve and Zed drove all night and morning to get here.

ALEX: Does this mean you're not mad at Steve anymore, Terra?

STEVE: Um . . .

TERRA: What happened in LA isn't important right now. What's important is that you get better.

ALEX: I have to go to the bathroom.

TERRA: Think you can handle it by yourself this time?

ALEX: I think so.

[bathroom door opening]

TERRA: Holler if you need any help.

[bathroom door closing]

STEVE: How much longer are they keeping him here?

TERRA: The doctor said another day or two.

STEVE: And his mom?

TERRA: Still no sign of her. I went back to the house yesterday 'cause I had to get a picture of her to e-mail the police.

STEVE: What about his brother?

TERRA: He was supposed to fly in last night but I haven't heard from him. I left him a message about their mom. I don't know.

TERRA: Steve, are things with you and Nathan still . . . I'm sorry.

STEVE: I'm the one who's sorry. You were right to—

UNIDENTIFIED MALE (distant): . . . *where's B612 . . . I'm looking for room . . .*

[curtain opening]

TERRA: Ronnie? You're R—

RONNIE: Where's Alex?

TERRA: He's in the bathroom.

RONNIE: Who's this?

STEVE: Um, I'm St—

[knocking on door]

RONNIE: Alex, it's me. Are you in there?

ALEX: *Ronnie?*

RONNIE: Hey bud, how ya doin'?

ALEX: *I can't poop.*

RONNIE: You can't poop.

TERRA: He's on a liquid diet. He hasn't had a bowel movement since—

RONNIE: Any word from the police?

TERRA: I haven't heard anything.

[toilet flushing]

[faucet running]

[bathroom door opening]

ALEX: RONNIE!

RONNIE: Hey bud, take it easy.

RONNIE: Let me see.

TERRA: Careful with the bandages.

RONNIE: What the—

RONNIE: Why are there two? Why did they cut here in the middle—

TERRA: They had to go in and feed everything through to make sure there wasn't any more damage to his intestine. We were lucky it wasn't a lot worse.

RONNIE: You call this lucky? What was he doing on that ladder in the first place?

ALEX: Ronnie, did you meet Steve too? He came with Zed who's outside with Carl Sagan. Let's go to the window, I'll show you—

RONNIE: OK, OK. There's that dog. And some bald hippie dude.

ALEX: I'm glad you came, Ronnie. I know you have meetings with prospective clients.

RONNIE: Of course, bud. I wanted to make sure you were all right.

RONNIE: Look, now that I'm here, you guys can—

TERRA: What is it?

RONNIE: I've seen you before. Where do I know you from?

ALEX: She's our half sis—

ALEX: Oops. I mean she's our Terra and we have the same dad.

RONNIE: We have the same . . .

TERRA: Ronnie—

RONNIE: Outside. Let's go.

TERRA: Just let me exp—

RONNIE: *Outside.*

TERRA: Here Steve, take his—

STEVE: Um . . .

[curtain closing]

ALEX: You can keep holding it, Steve.

STEVE: OK.

STEVE: I'll turn on the TV. What do you want to watch?

[channels flipping]

ALEX: What time's the Mars satellite launch? Can we watch the live stream?

STEVE: They postponed the launch because of high winds. They moved it to next week.

[cartoon music]

STEVE: How's this?

ALEX: OK.

ALEX: How's everyone on Rocketforum? Are you guys entering the new Civet Prize?

STEVE: I don't know. Everyone's—

RONNIE (distant): *Oh this is just . . . you spent a couple days with him and now you think . . .*

STEVE: We, um, have a lot of new members. I saw this article about how people are getting excited about astronomy and rocketry again because of CivSpace.

ALEX: That's good. Is Carl Sagan OK? He looked a little skinny. I can give him a bath when I'm out of the hospital, but can you guys feed him for—

RONNIE: *What do you mean you don't remember! Think! What'd you tell them . . .*

STEVE: Alex, wait. It's probably better if you stay in bed.

ALEX: But Ronnie and Terra are fighting. I don't want them to fight.

STEVE: I don't want them to fight either, but we should stay out of it right now. Your mom is . . .

ALEX: My mom is what?

STEVE: Ronnie and Terra are trying to find your mom.

ALEX: Is she OK?

STEVE: I'm sure she'll be—

[curtain opening]

STEVE: Terra . . .

TERRA: Stay here with Alex.

[keys jingling]

ALEX: Terra? Where's Ronnie and where's our mom? Where are you—

TERRA: Steve's going to stay here with you, I'll be back soon.

ALEX: Terra, don't leave! I don't want you to go . . .

TERRA: *Ronnie, wait!*

ALEX: Why are you guys . . .

ALEX: But . . .

STEVE: Um, I'm going to stop recording.

NEW RECORDING 41
5M 26S

Hi guys, I'm getting discharged from the hospital today. Discharged means I'm going home, like the hospital is the battery and I'm the energy and I'm leaving the battery so it's losing its charge. I guess that means when someone new gets here, the hospital gets recharged.

Ronnie was already here in my room when I woke up this morning. He was asleep in the chair by my bed and he was still wearing his suit and shirt from yesterday. I watched him sleep for a little while and then he yawned and rubbed his eyes, and then he asked me how long have I been awake and I told him just a few minutes. Then he asked me why am I staring at him and I told him, I'm just staring because I haven't seen you in person in so long.

Ronnie sat up in his chair a little bit and I asked him, What was all that stuff about yesterday? I told him that

Steve said him and Terra were trying to find our mom, so did they find her and is she OK? And Ronnie said they found her. He said she's in a hospital in Belmar and he's going to go see her in a little bit. I said, Why is Mom in a hospital, did she fall off a ladder too? and Ronnie said she's not hurt or anything, they just have to keep her at the hospital to run some tests. I asked him, What tests? and he said just some tests, they're not my concern, and I said I think they ARE my concern because that's how I'm feeling—concerned.

Then Ronnie scooted his chair closer to my bed and he smelled like the boys' locker room at my school, and he said he needs me to listen and think really clearly about something. I said, What is it? and he said he wants me to try to remember if there's anyone else who might know about me being at home by myself besides Terra and the guys, especially when our mom goes on her long walks.

I tapped my finger on my chin and I said, Hmm, let me think . . . , and then I told Ronnie there's Carl Sagan and Benji and my doctor here, Dr. Clemens, and Mr. Fogerty and Mrs. Campos at school and the older kid on the Amtrak train and Mr. Bashir at the gas station, and the Russells in Taos, New Mexico, and some of my other friends from Rocketforum.org, and also the intelligent beings I'm making these recordings for.

Ronnie looked like he'd seen a ghost when I told him

all that. Then he said from now on don't tell anyone else about our mom's walks or her quiet days or me being home alone, and don't tell anyone about going to SHARF and meeting strangers from the internet, and don't ever meet up with strangers in the first place!

I told Ronnie, I know, I'm sorry, and I asked him why shouldn't I talk about what happened though, does it have something to do with our mom's tests? and he said, Just don't. And then Ronnie said he has to go but the guys are on their way here, and Terra's coming later to sign me out from the hospital.

When Steve and Zed got here they helped me walk around in the hallways to keep moving like Dr. Clemens wanted, and after my walk we watched some TV together in my room but none of the shows I like were on. So we watched a game show where the contestants were trying to guess the calories in different breakfast foods and it made me SO hungry. I still can't eat solid food but I can eat things that are in between solid and liquid now. I can eat goos and squishy stuff like oatmeal and apple sauce but I can't get it à la mode because I'm not supposed to have dairy.

The whole time we were watching TV Steve was acting weird again, but it wasn't mad-weird and it wasn't the kind of weird he was when we first met Terra. He kept staring out the window like he was looking for something, or waiting for someone, maybe he was waiting for Terra, and sometimes he would watch the show again but he would frown at the parts where you were supposed to laugh.

I said, Hey Steve, if this game show is making you sad we can watch something else, and Steve said it's not that, and I said, Then what is it, did you and Nathan fight again? because one time at the beginning of sixth grade Benji was making fun of me in the lunchroom in front of his new friends and I started crying, but then on the bus he said he's sorry and then we went to his house to play video games because forgiveness is a virtue.

Steve said it's nothing, and then he smiled but I knew it was a pretend smile. I said, Steve, I know you're only pretend-smiling and you're really sad because it's making me sad, and then he said let's talk about something else. He said him and Zed gave Carl Sagan a bath this morning and I said, Really? how did you do it because Carl Sagan usually hates baths. Steve said for whatever reason Carl Sagan is really calm around Zed, and I said it's probably because Zed meditates and Carl Sagan can sense things like that. Zed said maybe we can all try meditating right now, and Steve said, Sure, why not, so we turned off the TV and Steve sat in the chair and Zed sat on the window-sill. I was already sitting in my bed.

Zed said we should all just feel what we feel, and I felt

excited because I'll be reunited with Carl Sagan soon and I felt hopeful because I hoped everything with my mom's tests would be OK, and then Steve got up and walked out of the room. After we meditated Zed asked me how do I feel now and I said I feel worried about Steve because I'm not sure why he's being like this all of a sudden. I asked Zed, How do you feel? and he said centered, and I said, In the center of what? and he said in the center of the universe, and I told him that makes no sense because the universe has no center, it's rapidly expanding in all directions.

NEW RECORDING 42
8M 19S

Do you know what skit—sch—schiz-o . . . phrenia is?
I'm not sure if I'm saying that right.

Schizophrenia is when you hear voices that only you can hear and sometimes the voices tell you to do things, and you can't tell the difference between real and not real. I asked Terra is it like having an imaginary friend, because I've never had one but when I was in first grade some of the other kids had imaginary friends, so does that mean they have schizophrenia too? Terra said no, it's OK for kids, but when you get older you outgrow it and it's only a problem if you're an adult and still can't tell the difference.

The reason my mom is in the hospital is because she has schizophrenia, and one of the voices told her it was a good idea to walk from our house all the way to Belmar and go into their big shopping mall and take off her clothes and take a bath in the fountain.

It took Terra a really long time to tell me about my mom. When I asked her when she came to sign me out of the hospital she said she'd tell me later, so I asked her later when we were in the car and she said she'd tell me when we got back to the house, so I asked her at the house and she finally told me.

I asked Terra, When can we go see my mom because I miss her and I want her to meet my Terra, and also I'm pretty good at solving problems so maybe I can help her solve her schizophrenia problem. Terra said she's sure my mom misses me too and the doctors there are working on it, my mom's getting better as we speak. She said I'll be able to visit my mom soon, she promises, and I told Terra, I can't wait to see my mom, and I'll make her favorite foods and bring them to her so she knows how much I love her.

Carl Sagan was really excited to see me get discharged from the hospital. He tried to jump on me as soon as he saw me come out of the sliding doors and I said, Be careful, boy! I have stitches! I hugged him and scratched behind his ears and then we drove back to our house in Terra's car, but when we got here I almost didn't recognize our dining room. There were a bunch of boxes piled up against the wall and it was like the guys's apartment in

LA except instead of being empty the boxes were filled with papers, and there were papers in stacks all over the table too.

I said, What the heck happened here, where did all of these boxes and papers come from? and Terra said Ronnie brought them up from the basement and she's been helping him go through them, they're my mom's old tax returns and medical records and things like that. I told her, My head hurts from just looking at all that stuff! and Terra said she knows what I mean, her head hurts too. I told her that she should take a break and come play outside with me and Carl Sagan, but she said that Ronnie wants me to stay inside, and if anyone calls or comes knocking at the door don't answer it. I asked her why can't I go outside, it's a beautiful day out! And she said she'll explain later.

So I threw Carl Sagan's ball around inside the house, and when he got tired of chasing it down the hallway we sat on the sofa and I asked him what happened after we lost him at Zelda's. I said, What kind of adventures did you have in Las Vegas? What was Janine Maplethorn like? and Did you make friends with any other people or dogs? And he just looked at me like, Can I sleep in your lap?

I said, OK boy, just don't push against my belly because it still feels weird, I'm not supposed to touch my stitches or staples even though they're SO itchy. So Carl

Sagan put his paws across my legs and his head down on his paws and he started falling asleep, and I scratched behind his ears and I told him, I'm really sorry I left you boy, I'm never going to leave you again, I promise, and I'll get you trained as a service dog so that way you can go anywhere I go and you'll never be alone for the rest of your life.

And then I started falling asleep too, I've been sleeping almost as much as Carl Sagan lately. And when I woke up it still looked sunny and beautiful out but inside the house it was dark and quiet, and Carl Sagan wasn't sleeping in my lap anymore. I said, Carl Sagan? Where are you, boy? And I didn't hear an answer but I did hear muffled voices coming from somewhere, and I looked out the living room window and I saw Steve and Terra talking in our driveway.

Zed came over from the other room and he was holding Carl Sagan, and they sat down on the sofa next to me and I asked Zed, What are Steve and Terra talking about out there and why do they both look so sad? Zed looked out the window too, and we both watched Steve and Terra talking for a while, and then Zed said that they're having a long-overdue conversation.

I asked him, What do you mean? Have they been out there a long time? And Zed said that he means they're talking about something they've both been holding in for too long.

And then he told me that Steve broke up with his girlfriend. Steve did it that last morning we were in LA, before the big fight.

I said, Wow, what made him do that? And Zed told me he asked Steve the same question, and Steve said that it was because of meeting me and Terra, that our trip to SHARF and Las Vegas made him see what a crummy relationship he had, and he didn't want to have it anymore.

I said, So Steve broke up with his girlfriend, and THEN he got the flowers to give to Terra?

And Zed said, That's right, and I asked him, Then was that Steve's sacrifice? because Terra said that real love means a sacrifice, but a good kind of sacrifice, that's about giving up something to get a bigger something else. So did Steve give up his girlfriend because he loves Terra?

Zed looked at me and then back out the window, and he said, This is Steve's sacrifice, right now. He said Steve's telling Terra how he really feels about her, knowing that she might not feel the same way.

And I looked out the window too and I said, He's telling her the truth, and Zed said, She's telling *him* the truth as well. And I didn't know what they were saying to each other because I don't know how to read lips, but it looked like they're both trying to be brave.

And I wanted to go record it for you guys. I wanted to finally get my man in love. But Zed said I should stay inside. I asked him, Why? Why should I do that, Zed? I know Ronnie wants me to stay indoors and pretend I'm not home if someone knocks or calls, but nobody's telling me why, and this whole time I've been trying to get a man in love and now he's right there in the driveway and this is my chance, and now you don't want me to go outside either!

And Zed said, You already have it.

I told him No, I don't, I have Steve talking on the phone to his girlfriend from before but that wasn't the right thing! And then Zed said, You already have it, it's just not what you thought it was, it's even better than that, and I said, That makes no sense, Zed! Are you even listening to what I'm saying? And then Zed was really quiet, and I looked out the window again and I saw Steve and Terra hug each other but then they still looked sad. I guess it didn't work.

Steve started walking down the street, and Terra came inside and she was crying, and she went in my room and shut the door and then even Zed looked sad. I said, Why are you sad too, it's making me sad, and then he just hugged me. I asked Zed, Do you think there are intelligent beings out there in the cosmos who don't have sadness? and he said he doesn't know, and when he said it I could feel his voice rumbling through his chest.

Then I wondered . . . do YOU GUYS have sadness?

Maybe you've figured out a way to get rid of it, or maybe instead of sadness you have something else.

Maybe your sadness is our happiness, and you laugh and smile when you're sad and it makes you feel good and it's like how whales sound like they're crying but that's just how they sound all the time, even when they're having fun.

Or maybe you're always sad, and you have three hearts and one lung and sadness is what keeps your hearts beating and your lung breathing. It's what keeps you alive.

I told Zed my ideas and then Zed started crying and I started crying, but it didn't feel like only sadness, it felt like something else too. And then I fell asleep again and when I woke up I was here in my bed.

NEW RECORDING 43
8M 46S

Everyone is being really weird today. Nobody will tell me anything!

This morning I asked Ronnie can I see our mom today and he said I can't, and I said, Why not, YOU went to see her yesterday so why can't I go see her today? I told him, Terra said I'll be able to see our mom soon and it's already soon and if we wait any longer it won't be soon anymore. Ronnie said he doesn't want to talk about it, and I said, How are we supposed to help her schizophrenia if we don't even talk about it! And then Terra said we should let Ronnie get back to work.

I told Terra, I know that the doctors are helping my mom get better and she's on medication because you told me that already, but I want to help too. I said, I'm sure there are some things that the doctors don't know about my mom because nobody told them. Terra said she's sorry, everyone's doing their best, and I said, Well clearly it's not good enough! And then Ronnie told me to quiet down, he's trying to focus.

Not only wouldn't Ronnie and Terra tell me anything, everyone was in a bad mood too, even the weather was in a bad mood. It was cloudy and gloomy and whenever Steve and Terra talked to each other they would say just a couple words and then one or both of them would frown, and it made me not want to be around them.

I think it made Zed feel the same way because he asked me can he borrow my computer, he wants to write down some thoughts that he had last night, and then he was in my room typing for hours. He didn't even have dinner! We ordered pizza for everyone and a banana smoothie for me because I'm still on a semi-liquid diet, and when the food got here I went to get him and I said, Hey Zed, are you doing a vow of not eating now too? But he didn't hear me, he was too busy typing.

We couldn't eat in the dining room because the table was still covered with papers and Ronnie's laptop and stuff, he was sitting there all day researching the State of Colorado website and calling people on his phone. So we just ate in the kitchen. We stood around the pizza boxes on the counter and everyone was really quiet and nobody was eating their pizza, and I said, I know why Steve's not eating but why is everyone else not eating too? And Terra said it's because there are so many outstanding questions. I told her it's great to ask outstanding questions because that's how you get outstanding answers so let's hear them. She said that outstanding also means leftover, so by outstanding questions she means there are a bunch of leftover questions that still don't have answers.

Terra said that one of the outstanding questions is that my mom's hospital costs a lot of money and so did my trip to the emergency room, and our insurance doesn't cover everything. I said that's a statement, not a question, and she said the question is, How are we going to pay for it all? I told Terra I'm sorry I cost so much money, I promise I'll work overtime at Mr. Bashir's gas station and make some money to pay for my emergency room and my mom's hospital also, and then Ronnie said let's not talk about this, and I said, You never want to talk about anything! You never want to talk about our dad and now you don't want to talk about our mom either! And then Ronnie went back to the dining room and Steve and Terra both looked sad again, and nobody said anything for a long time. Zed was still in my room typing.

Finally Terra said let's watch *Contact* because we didn't finish it and she wants to see the rest, and I thought that was a good idea because it's better than everyone frowning or being mad at each other. So we put the outstanding pizza in the refrigerator and I put on *Contact*.

We got to the part where Dr. Arroway is in the meeting room and she already has government approval to buy time at the Very Large Array, she just needs the money now, and then the guy in the meeting room tells her, You have your money. When we got to that part, I paused it because I had to go to the bathroom, and then I had my first bowel movement! It smelled like a dead cat. It smelled SO bad.

When I came back after my bowel movement everyone was standing around the dining table, even Zed, and Ronnie was saying, It's never going to work, nobody's going to do that. I said, Nobody's going to do what? and Terra said Steve just came up with a great idea for how we can pay for some of the hospital bills.

Steve's idea was that we should tell everyone on Rocketforum what happened and ask them to donate money to help. He said, I'm not sure if it'll work but everyone loves Alex, and if they're each willing to chip in ten or twenty bucks it'll make things a little easier at least. I said, Oh, you mean like finding sponsors for me instead of a rocket, and Steve said that's exactly it. I asked him if I get sponsors does that mean I have to paint their logos on my body, and Zed laughed and Terra said I don't have to if I don't want to, and I said, Whew, that's a relief.

Ronnie said we don't need anyone's help, he'll figure

out a way to pay for everything on his own, and Terra said, Let's just try it, what do we have to lose! She said that Steve's right, and Ronnie has other more important things to focus on right now, and Steve smiled a little but then he frowned again, and I said, What things? You mean with our mom? and Ronnie said he still doesn't think it'll work. But Steve and Zed both thought it was a great idea and I thought it was a pretty good idea so Ronnie said, Fine, but let's not get our hopes up. I told him I agree, we should keep them in the middle.

Steve said he'll start working on a new post right away, and he went on my computer and started writing the post, and Ronnie went back on his laptop, and the rest of us finished watching *Contact*. After the movie was over Terra said it was so good, it was refreshing to see an intelligent female scientist as the main character. Zed said one thing he loves about *Contact* and about *Cosmos* is they show how science can be deeply spiritual too. He said that a writer he really likes once said that most religions started off being based on science, only it was the best science that they had at that time, and I said, Huh, it really makes you think. And then right when we were about to watch the Blu-ray bonus features Steve came out and said he finished the Rocketforum post.

The post that Steve wrote was SO long, guys. It was about me and my Golden iPod and everything that happened to us after SHARF but without all the parts about the fighting because Rocketforum is a family-friendly forum. Steve asked me can he take a picture of me and Terra and of my scars to prove to everyone that he's not making it up, because sometimes people don't believe what they read on the internet. He said also it would be great if we could upload some of my recordings from the Golden iPod and share those too, but mostly the ones from SHARF, definitely not the ones from Vegas or afterwards, and Terra said that's another great idea.

After we uploaded my recordings Steve set up the page where everyone could go to donate money, and he showed us when he was done, and it even had a little bar that shows what percent we are to the goal. Terra and me read it all over one more time to make sure there weren't any spelling mistakes, then Ronnie read it over too and told Steve to take out all the stuff about the ladder and just say I got into an accident. I asked Ronnie why and he said it's a family matter, and I said, Does it have something to do with our mom? and then Ronnie didn't want to talk about it again.

I told Terra, I'm glad we're doing something about this outstanding question but what about all your guys's other outstanding questions? I said I have my own outstanding questions too, like When can I see my mom? and What kind of shows do they have at her hospital?

and Why doesn't Ronnie want me to go see her and why don't you or Ronnie want to talk about stuff? Why can't you guys just tell me the truth! And then Terra frowned again and she STILL wouldn't talk about it.

I don't know why everyone is being such a bleep. I wish I was sixteen already because then I could drive a car and go see my mom by myself and I wouldn't need Ronnie or Terra to take me. Maybe Steve was right with what he said in LA—no one wants to tell me the truth because I'm just a kid.

But then what am I supposed to do?

What do you guys do?

Won't SOMEbody answer my questions?

NEW RECORDING 44
39S

TERRA: Alex, look. I'm recording.

TERRA: Don't you want to say something to them?

TERRA: Don't you want to tell them about your plans for Voyager 4?

TERRA: Tell them about how supportive everyone on Rocketforum's been. At least do that. We're almost a third of the way to our goal! They're doing it for you, Alex. Isn't that exciting?

TERRA: Alex, you can't just not say anything.

TERRA: I know you want to see your mom. I know you miss her.

TERRA: It's just that she's not . . . ready.

TERRA: We'll take you to see her, just not right now. She needs time to get better.

TERRA: Alex—

NEW RECORDING 45
2M 18S

Alex still won't talk. Now he's locked himself in his mom's room. He's already been in there for most of the day.

This morning while we were having breakfast he kept crying and asking when he could see her, even more than before. He just wouldn't let it go. And the questions became demands, like, I want to see her NOW.

She's not under watch anymore, which is promising. But Ronnie said she's still not entirely herself. How can we let Alex see his mom in that condition?

I tried to reason with him but he just covered his ears and kept yelling *now now now*, he wants to see her *now*. He wasn't crying anymore but this—this was somehow worse. The guys and I tried getting him to play with Carl Sagan, with his rocket stuff, everything. I asked him to tell me more about his tesseract, but he wasn't interested in that either. And Ronnie is adamant about him not going outside because of everything that's happening with CPS or DHS or whatever they call Child Protective Services here. We can't risk them coming by and seeing Alex, and taking him away. Putting him in a foster home. Nothing we're doing is really helping though. Alex probably feels like he's under house arrest . . .

I called Donna again—called my mom. I told her about what's been going on with Ronnie and their mom, and with CPS and how Alex is refusing to come out of the room. I told her everything, even what happened in LA with Steve. And I said maybe it was a mistake not being up-front with Alex from the beginning because, I mean, I know how much he values honesty, values the truth. I know how much Alex loves his mom. And I want him to see her, I really do, but I'm just afraid that . . . what I mean is . . . there are things we want to protect him from, Ronnie and I both. There are things we don't want Alex to have to learn the hard way.

Anyway, I blabbed on and on about that stuff and Donna was pretty quiet the whole time, and then I asked her what she thought about all of it and it took her a moment to answer. And then, out of the blue, she said she's proud of me.

I was like, Proud of me? And she was like, Yes, proud

of me for being there for Alex and keeping him safe. I said, Then why does it feel like I'm failing him all the time?

And she said, and I keep thinking about this—she said, It's because you love him.

It's because . . .

NEW RECORDING 46
29M 18S

RONNIE: What'd you say?

[cars passing]

ALEX: I'm recording now, is that OK?

RONNIE: Yeah, OK.

ALEX: Hi guys. We're on the highway driving back to our house right now. Last night Ronnie finally said he's going to take me to see our mom tomorrow which is today and we just saw her. I wanted Terra to come too but Terra said that I should go with Ronnie, she'll meet my mom some other time.

Do you guys have hospitals where you are? Do you have different hospitals for different things? I thought my mom's hospital in Belmar was going to be like the one I was in after I fell off the ladder but it wasn't. It's a behavioral health hospital.

When we got there the lady at the front desk told us

just to wait in the lobby, a tech will come get us when our mom is ready. I asked her, What's a tech, is it some kind of technology like a robot, so is a robot going to take us to see our mom? And she said tech stands for technician, which means someone who works at the hospital but isn't a nurse or a doctor.

While we were waiting Ronnie got a phone call from his prospective client and then he went outside to talk, and I wanted to see what kinds of stuff they had at a behavioral health hospital so I walked down one of the hallways, and it looked more like the hallways at my school except there were no lockers. I saw some patients and they were wearing normal clothes, not hospital gowns, but I could tell they were patients because they were wearing plastic ID bracelets like I had to wear in my hospital. One of the rooms I saw was called Day Room and it had a TV and there were patients inside watching TV, and there was another Day Room with round tables and patients at the tables coloring in coloring books, which I did in kindergarten, so I thought that maybe when people go to the behavioral health hospital it's like they have to start over from when they're born and learn how to crawl and walk and talk and go to kindergarten and everything so they remember how to behave like grown-ups.

Those weren't the only rooms I saw though. There were other rooms that had two beds in them and pictures and decorations on the walls, and there was a room with just one bed and no decorations and the bed had big belts like in *Frankenstein,* and then a guy with a clipboard came up to me and asked me am I lost. I told him, No, I'm just looking around because my brother's outside talking on the phone and we're waiting to see my mom and are you a tech? He said he is, and I should go wait in the lobby, and he took me back there and then Ronnie got mad at me—

RONNIE: I thought I'd lost you, OK? You can't just go wandering off without telling me.

ALEX: I know, I'm sorry I wandered off, Ronnie. I was just curious . . .

RONNIE: Just try not to do anything like that again.

ALEX: OK . . .

ALEX: Hey Ronnie, do you know if our mom's room is like that *Frankenstein* room I saw? I bet they use lightning in there to help patients—

RONNIE: They don't do that kind of treatment anymore.

ALEX: Well, next time we go we should visit her in her room instead of the cafeteria, and we should bring some of her things like her slippers and an extra pillow because the ones in the rooms I saw looked flat. We should bring her pictures to hang on the wall too, that way it'll feel more like home.

RONNIE: Let's hold off on that for—

ALEX: But she probably misses all her stuff!

RONNIE: Look, you saw how she was today. Maybe when she's herself again.

ALEX: What do you mean when she's herself? She's not NOT herself, she just has her schizophrenia problem, and if we bring her all her stuff we can help her get better.

RONNIE: It doesn't really work like that, bud.

ALEX: Then how does it work?

ALEX: How does it work, Ronnie?

[cars passing]

ALEX: Ronnie's talking about what happened when we saw our mom. After we waited in the lobby they told us we can meet her in the cafeteria, and we went there and then our mom came out with another tech, a big guy, he was SO tall, and he stood by the wall the whole time we were talking. Ronnie asked our mom, How do you feel? and she was looking at Ronnie with really big eyes, and then she looked at me with really big eyes, and I wanted to hold her hand and make her hair not all messy but she didn't want me to touch her. So I just said I love you and I hope you get better.

My mom was definitely having one of her quiet days. Except maybe this time it was one of the voices in her head that told her she wasn't supposed to talk, or maybe one of the voices was talking a lot so she couldn't pay attention to it and to us at the same time.

But then she finally did talk, and she said, I'm not telling you anything, you're not my sons. I thought it was weird, like, What more proof do you need! We're right here! And I tried to convince my mom that I was really me, so I told her something that only we would know about. I said, Remember that time you picked me up from choir practice after school when I was in third grade and I was the only boy who was a soprano because my voice is so high, and when we were driving back I had to poop really bad and I was trying to hold it in and hold it in and I even turned around and stood on my knees on the seat because it made me want to go less, but then I couldn't hold it in any longer and I pooped my pants right before we got to the house and I was crying, but you cleaned me and kissed me and you said it's nothing to be embarrassed about because even adults do it sometimes, and isn't it funny that when the poop is inside of us we don't think it's disgusting but when it's on the outside then it's disgusting?

I thought for sure that my mom would hear that and know I was really me. But after I told her, my mom said, You're not Alex, you're an alien, you stole my memories and you're using them against me. And I told her I'm not, or at least I don't THINK I'm an alien, and besides, it's unlikely that aliens would come to steal our memories because we haven't even found intelligent life outside our own—

RONNIE: Alex, you have to realize—it doesn't matter what we say. She's not going to believe us. Not when she's like that.

ALEX: But she had some really interesting ideas though. Like when she told the big tech we're only pretending to be her sons and we're really made of trees sent by the aliens. I've never heard that in my whole entire life! Although my hero did say every living thing is made of starstuff so in a way we ARE trees and trees are us, even though we probably weren't—

RONNIE: Alex, Mom's not right.

ALEX: She's not wrong.

RONNIE: That's not— What I mean is that even if they're interesting ideas to you, they're not normal for her. You can see that, right? She's not herself. You remember when she used to go on those shopping sprees? I'd come home from class and there'd be shopping bags full of coffeemakers and jewelry, Louis Vuitton bags. That one time you were playing an Xbox—

ALEX: I liked the Xbox.

RONNIE: I know you did, bud. And I'm sorry you couldn't keep it. But my point is the condition she's in right now—it's ten times worse than that.

ALEX: Maybe the medicine they're giving her isn't working.

RONNIE: You heard what Dr. Hewitt said. They're still

testing out different medications. Trying to find the right combination for her. It takes time.

ALEX: But why can't it be at home?

RONNIE: What do you mean?

ALEX: You said it's going to take time for them to find the right combination of medicine, so why can't she just spend that time at home? Can't she take her medicine there too?

RONNIE: She needs to be someplace where they can keep an eye on her. Where there's someone to take care of her around the clock.

ALEX: But I can do that. I can keep an eye on her and take care of her around the clock. I'll drink lots of Steve's LOX and stay awake and that way I can take care of her.

RONNIE: I'm sorry Alex, but you can't. It's not possible.

ALEX: There's always a chance! And besides, they don't even have the food that she likes in the cafeteria!

RONNIE: What if she's still like this in a couple months? Have you thought about that? You have school.

ALEX: I can do homeschool. Benji told me that Brianna Fischer's parents are going to homeschool her when she finishes eighth—

RONNIE: It's more complicated than that. And there are some legal—

ALEX: Why do you and Terra keep saying that? I can understand complicated stuff. I figured out how to build a rocket and go to New Mexico, so I can figure out this too. Do you think I can't understand?

RONNIE: Look, it's not that I think you can't—

[tires squealing]

RONNIE: SON OF A—

[horn honking repeatedly]

RONNIE: —USE YOUR SIGNAL!

RONNIE: Some people . . .

ALEX: I wish Dad was still here.

RONNIE: No you don't.

ALEX: He would've made Mom feel better.

RONNIE: You don't know anything about Dad.

ALEX: I know some stuff. I know he was a civil engineer and he wore—

RONNIE: You don't know the whole story.

ALEX: That's because you never tell me the whole story! Why don't you ever want to talk about our dad? Mom always said he was a good man at heart. She said he loved us very much and—

RONNIE: Mom was trying to protect you. And Mom, she had a blind spot when it came to him.

ALEX: Was it her schizophren—

RONNIE: She couldn't see him for who he really was.

ALEX: Who was he really?

ALEX: Ronnie?

ALEX: Who was he really? Terra said he threw base-balls really hard. She said his whiskers tickled her chin.

RONNIE: Terra didn't spend the kind of time with him that Mom and I did. She didn't see what I saw. What Terra saw was only the surface. A skin. Deep down he was selfish and abusive.

ALEX: Did he hit Mom with a hockey stick like Benji's dad hit his mom?

RONNIE: What? No. Benji's dad— What?

ALEX: That's why Benji's parents got divorced.

RONNIE: I didn't know that.

ALEX: So then our dad—

RONNIE: Dad never hit Mom, at least not that I know of.

RONNIE: He never hit me either, but he came really close once—while Mom was pregnant with you. I ran away from home for three days—well, more like hid in Justin Mendoza's basement for three days. Justin would sneak food down for me at breakfast and dinner. But then one morning while he was at school, his mom came downstairs to do laundry and found me.

ALEX: But . . . why would you run away?

RONNIE: I don't remember the exact reason. It was probably something dumb. I just couldn't stand being in the same house with the two of them sometimes. And man, Dad was furious. They'd reported me missing and everything. He started yelling and undoing his belt and Mom was trying to shield me, and he kept telling her to get out of the way. And I was like, Go ahead. Go ahead, hit me, I'll call the cops. I'll run away for good. But he ended up just locking me in my room. I was glad too, because it meant that I didn't have to see his sorry face.

RONNIE: You know, just 'cause he never hit us doesn't mean he wasn't abusive in other ways. Mom got the worst of it. Whenever they got into a fight he'd tell her it was her fault, that she wasn't as thin or pretty as she used to be—

ALEX: But . . .

RONNIE: —she kicked him out a bunch of times but he always managed to talk his way back in. She'd threaten to leave him but he'd apologize, say he'd never do it again. Same stuff you see on TV. You'd think that after seeing that enough times you'd recognize a bad situation but no, it's the opposite. It only gives you these roles to play out. He was a bully, Alex. Dad was just a huge bully.

ALEX: But . . . they met at Mom's bank and he asked her out to dinner! They went on top of Mount Sam and had their first kiss and looked at the stars and fell in lov—

RONNIE: They met in a bar.

ALEX: What?

RONNIE: Mom didn't start working at the bank until much later. And they never went up to Mount Sam together. I remember 'cause she took me up there on the tram once and she told me it was her first time going up there. Mom and Dad met in a bar.

ALEX: That's not true—

RONNIE: It's what happened. I'm sorry it wasn't on Mount Sam, Alex. But it's what happened.

ALEX: But . . .

RONNIE: See, that's exactly what I mean. Mom would always try to paint him in this more romantic light. She made up that story because—because she didn't want to admit to the bad stuff that was happening. I should've known she was never serious about leaving him. There's no way she could have gone through with it, with divorce, and he knew it. He would just take advantage—

RONNIE: Are you crying?

ALEX: I'm . . . not . . .

[sniffling]

RONNIE: Look, bud, I'm really sorry you have to hear it this way . . .

RONNIE: But if you want the truth, Alex, the truth is that Dad wasn't totally faithful to Mom. He was a cheater. A bully and a cheater. And it started happening long before you were born. There's nothing you could've—

ALEX: I'm glad she didn't divorce him . . .

RONNIE: You're glad—

ALEX: Because if she did then I wouldn't exist.

RONNIE: ——

[sniffling]

ALEX: Is that how come we're related to Terra?

RONNIE: Dad traveled a lot for work. I don't know if Mom ever told you how much he traveled, but it was a lot. He'd leave all the time to go visit building sites. He probably just met Terra's mom on one of his trips to Vegas and . . .

ALEX: And what?

RONNIE: Got her pregnant. And we figured out why his name came up in the marriage index, Terra and I. Her mom said they did get married but it got annulled right away.

ALEX: What does annulled—

RONNIE: It got canceled. Because he was already married to Mom. I have no clue what could've been going through his head when—

ALEX: Does that mean we could have more half sisters and half brothers?

RONNIE: More . . . Man, I don't even want to think about that right now . . .

RONNIE: It's just—I remember how he was with everyone. They all loved him. At parties he'd be the one with the biggest circle of people around him. From the outside he was the perfect husband, the perfect father, and I was so mad at him for that. It was like, these people don't know. They have no clue what he's really like.

RONNIE: I remember once, he took me to Safeway—this was when Lolo and Lola were flying in from the Philippines. Mom ran out of milk or pineapples or something, and he took me to get more. I was probably around your age then—ten, eleven. Maybe a little younger. I went to the cereal aisle to grab my Wheaties and when I came back to the cart he was talking to some girl. She was really young, maybe in college. She had streaked blond hair and she was laughing at everything he said. And I remember—I remember seeing the way Dad was talking to this girl and knowing deep down that something wasn't right. He was using the same voice he'd use with Mom sometimes, on the good days. When things were OK. The girl saw me and tried to say hello but I didn't know how to respond. She reeked of some kind of strawberry perfume—to this day I can't stand that smell. And then she laughed and wrote down her number and Dad put it in his wallet, and after she walked away Dad just had this dumb grin on his face. He was like, Look at that, we made a new friend. He said we should keep our new friend our little secret, and then on the way home he bought me ice cream.

[turn signal clicking]

[tires on gravel]

ALEX: Why are we stopping?

RONNIE: I need to stop.

[engine shutting off]

[cars passing]

RONNIE: You wanna know the worst part?

RONNIE: Mom was in such a good mood that night with Lolo and Lola here. During dinner everyone was talking and laughing. Having a great time. It was probably one of the happiest family dinners we'd ever had, and then, in the middle of all that—I remember—Dad looked over at me, and he WINKED at me.

RONNIE: He only cared about himself, Alex. I knew it even then too. Maybe not consciously, but I knew it. And I just wanted to—I don't know, do SOMETHING. Call him out on it.

RONNIE: I don't believe it . . .

ALEX: What is it?

RONNIE: I've never told anyone about that.

ALEX: Not even Lauren?

RONNIE: Not even Lauren.

ALEX: But she's your girlfriend, you're supposed to tell her everything.

RONNIE: I don't need to expose her to that.

ALEX: Is that why you never bring her home for Thanksgiving or Christmas?

RONNIE: No, it's—

ALEX: Or do you not want to expose her to me either.

RONNIE: Hey, listen. Of course I want her to meet you. I tell her about you all the time.

ALEX: You do?

RONNIE: You bet I do. I tell her about how smart and imaginative you are. How interested you are in science and astronomy. How you can already cook for yourself and Mom.

RONNIE: You'll meet her someday.

RONNIE: It's just—I hate him so much sometimes. For what he did to Mom, how he made her feel. And he made me hate *her* for not leaving him after all the stuff he pulled. I was like, How can you let him keep doing this! How can you stay with him!

RONNIE: I wished he were dead. I wished for it when I blew out my birthday candles. I thought if he were dead, then we could finally move on. Once he was gone for good, we'd be free. We could live normal lives.

RONNIE: But then when I picked up the phone and it was his foreman, saying there'd been an accident . . .

RONNIE: I didn't see it coming, that feeling. I felt the same chill when Terra called me and told me you were in the hospital. Thing is—I actually felt sorry for him. I couldn't believe I felt that way. It scared me that after all that, I still . . .

ALEX: You still loved him.

RONNIE: I still loved him . . .

RONNIE: You know, I had to break the news to Mom, and Mom—Mom wasn't good. She wasn't as bad as right now but she wasn't good. She kept saying how she needed him to protect her, to protect her from the bad people. She was hysterical, I thought she was just really shaken. I had no idea that it might've been . . .

ALEX: That it might've been schizophrenia?

RONNIE: That it might've been schizophrenia.

RONNIE: She got better, over time, but she wasn't really the same after that. She kept the box with his ashes in her room. I told her to put it away, and take down his pictures because they were only torturing her, but she always said no. We'd get into fights over it. It's like she didn't *want* to get better.

RONNIE: Then one night she fell asleep in your bed— she came to read you a story and fell asleep next to you, and I was lying awake and the impulse, it just hit me. I went in her room and grabbed the box with his ashes. I took it under my arm—it was surprising how heavy it was—and I got my bike and didn't even think about where I was going. I just knew I had to get that box out of the house. I rode down the hill and kept riding and I came to a construction site. There's that subdivision there now— the one off Mill Road—but back then it was just a plot of dirt. And I went into the middle of the dirt and dumped all his ashes on the ground and I kicked them and kicked them and made them all disappear.

RONNIE: The next day I kept waiting for Mom to say

something, but she never did. She never once brought up that the ashes were missing. I never asked her why . . .

RONNIE: Look, I know his death was an accident. I know that. But it was like he did it on purpose, you know? Like he left us on purpose. He made us depend on him, he made Mom depend on him, and then he just left.

ALEX: But you left too, Ronnie. You went to California.

RONNIE: I . . .

ALEX: And Benji's dad left him and his mom and sister. And I left Carl Sagan even though I didn't mean to, and now we're leaving Mom in the behavioral health hospital.

RONNIE: We're not—that's different. That's temporary.

RONNIE: Maybe . . . Maybe Benji's dad left because he knew that if he stayed, he'd end up hurting Benji and his mom again. Maybe that's why. Maybe he couldn't trust himself.

ALEX: He had to make a sacrifice?

RONNIE: That's right. He had to do what was best for his family, even if that meant that he wouldn't get to see them. Even if it hurt him that he wouldn't get to be with them. He had to take responsibility—*real* responsibility—for his actions. That's what it means to be an adult.

ALEX: So then, when we really love someone, we have to sacrifice getting to be with them?

RONNIE: No, not always. Not usually. But sometimes . . . sometimes it's the only way. Sometimes when we really love someone we have to leave them, because it's better for them than if we stayed.

ALEX: It's like how we have to go to Mars.

RONNIE: What?

ALEX: So the earth is dying because of things that we did, right? Things that humans did. And we KEEP hurting it, and the forests are disappearing and the oceans are rising and animals are going extinct, so maybe that's why we have to colonize Mars. We have to leave Earth so Earth can get better again.

RONNIE: That's . . .

RONNIE: Bud, listen. I'm sorry I left. It wasn't because I don't love you and Mom—I absolutely do. It was just the only way for us to . . . I mean, I couldn't stay here. In Rockview. I couldn't let it beat me, do you understand? I had to live my own life, and I—I know I haven't been the best about visiting, and I wasn't here when you needed me. I know that now. I haven't been the best role model for you but I'm—I'm just trying to be a good person. I'm just trying to do the right—

RONNIE: Are you crying again?

RONNIE: What are you crying for?

ALEX: Because you're crying.

RONNIE: ——

ALEX: Ronnie?

RONNIE: What is it?

ALEX: I've never seen you cry before.

RONNIE: ——

RONNIE: Alex . . . Listen, bud, Terra and I have been trying to shield you from this . . . but I want you to know what's happening. That call I took earlier—that wasn't for work. That was someone from DHS—Department of Human Services. They've been investigating our family, and that's why I've been telling you to stay inside, I've been trying to protect—

ALEX: I know.

RONNIE: You know?

ALEX: I listened to Terra's recordings.

RONNIE: Why didn't you say anything?

ALEX: Because I was waiting for YOU to tell me. I'm NOT a little kid anymore, Ronnie. I'm not in elementary school anymore and it's not like when we still slept in the same room, and I know that the truth is uncomfortable but if I'm only happy all the time then it's not bravery!

RONNIE: ——

ALEX: Um . . . why are you looking at me like that?

RONNIE: Because I haven't seen you in a long time.

ALEX: ——

RONNIE: I know how much you want to know the truth about everything, Alex. I really do, bud. It's just you have to understand that sometimes it's hard for people— it's hard for ME—because you're still my little bro. You're still Alex. It's my job to make sure you don't get hurt, and I haven't been doing my job lately.

ALEX: But Ronnie, I can handle it. I can take care of myself.

RONNIE: I see that now. You're a tough kid. I just need you to try and be a little more patient with me, and I'll try not to hold stuff back. Deal?

ALEX: Deal.

RONNIE: Good man.

ALEX: So what do we do now? Are you going to move back home?

RONNIE: We can talk about that, but first we gotta deal with this DHS situation. That's more immediate.

[car starting]

ALEX: But what about—

RONNIE: Let's discuss it back at the house. I want Terra and the guys to be there too.

ALEX: Will we really talk about it this time?

RONNIE: Yes.

ALEX: Everything?

RONNIE: Yes.

[tires on gravel]

[engine accelerating]

NEW RECORDING 47
4M 32S

Guys I have big big big news news news! CivSpaceScott donated fifty dollars to help pay for my hospital bill and so did CivSpaceElisa, and they showed the forum thread to the people at their work and they donated a bunch also and Lander Civet sent me a message! THE Lander Civet!

His message said that Dr. Carl Sagan is one of his all-time heroes too, and when he was a kid he got to meet him and shake his hand. Lander said he has an exact replica of the Voyager Golden Record in his office and he read about my Golden iPod in the forum post and listened to some of my recordings, and he would be honored if me and my family would join him as his special guests to watch the Mars satellite launch at Cape Canaveral, do I want to come?

I messaged Lander back right away and I told him,

Are you kidding me! Of course we want to come to the launch, DUH! And Lander said that's great, he can't wait to meet me, and his assistant is going to help us book our tickets for Florida and everything.

I wanted us all to go to Johnny Rockets to celebrate because Dr. Clemens said I can eat solid food now that I've had my first bowel movement. And Ronnie said we'll go celebrate soon but not today, not right now, right now we need to talk about DHS and his plan for our family. He said one of their social workers is coming over to our house the day after tomorrow, and I said, What's a social worker, is it someone whose job it is to go on Twitter? And Ronnie said it's not, it's just a person that works for the state, and Zed said it's also someone who tries to help people in need. I said, Oh, in that case I'm a social worker too, and Ronnie said, Let's focus.

He said that the only real solution he sees is for me to go live with him in California for now and he'll start looking for a bigger apartment, and then when our mom gets better enough to come out of the hospital we'll move her out there too and we'll sell our house in Rockview. I said, But what about your condo? and Ronnie said it's not his, he can't afford a condo on a junior agent's salary so he's just renting it, and it's only a single room in the back of someone else's property and it doesn't even have its own kitchen. Then I said, But what about my school and Benji and my job for Mr. Bashir, and who's going to be president of the Rockview Planetary Society and why can't YOU just move back from LA and live at home? And then I started crying a little again.

Terra held my hand and she said she knows it's going to be hard, but Ronnie's job is in LA and he's already making a lot of sacrifices, and now it's up to me to make some sacrifices too. She said I can always chat with Benji online and maybe he can take over as president of the Rockview Planetary Society, and there are gas stations in California too. Ronnie said he already talked to the guys about it and they've agreed to watch me if he has to travel for work, and I looked at the guys and Steve nodded, and Zed said it's true. Ronnie said also Terra's only going to be a few hours away in Las Vegas, and I asked him, Do you have an air mattress? and he said he doesn't, and I said, Can you get one because if you have an air mattress then Terra can come live with us too and sleep on the air mattress. And Ronnie and Terra looked at each other and then Ronnie said let's talk more about that later, for now let's just get through the next couple of days.

I asked Ronnie what does all this have to do with the social worker and he said that it's going to raise some red flags if we just leave the state suddenly, and we don't want them to think that I need to be in a foster home.

I asked him, So how do we raise some green flags? and he said that's exactly why this meeting is so important, because if we show them I have a safe environment right now, then they'll leave us alone and we can do what we want. Ronnie said that's why before the social worker comes over we have to get everything with the house in good order. I said, What do you mean, I keep the house in pretty good order already, and Ronnie said yeah but what about the unmowed lawn and the old coupon flyers in our mom's room, and the dust and wet dog smell, and the stains on the living room carpet from before I found out about Carl Sagan's digestive problems, and I said touché. Ronnie said we'll have to take care of all that stuff anyway if we're going to sell the house, so we might as well do it now. He said let's just have a quiet dinner at home and clean up what we can tonight, and then we'll get started on everything else first thing in the morning. So that's what we're doing.

I have to get back to cleaning now, guys. I'll record more for you soon.

NEW RECORDING 48
5M 37S

I. Am. So. Exhausted.

But it's a different kind of exhausted than I was right after my accident. Then my whole body was sore and all I wanted to do was sleep. Now my body's tired but so is my brain, it's almost like I've been running a mile and trying to solve a really hard riddle at the same time.

Everyone else is really exhausted too, but they're all still cleaning. The guys came over this morning and Ronnie went to Justin Mendoza's house to borrow his lawnmower because ours doesn't work anymore, and he came back and filled it with gas and he pulled the cord and it went *blub blub blub bvvvuuuuuuu* and Carl Sagan started crying because he was scared of the noise. But then he got used to it.

Ronnie pushed the lawnmower for a while and then he let me try, but it was SO heavy. So Ronnie pushed it again and the bag would get full really quickly, and every time it got full I helped him dump the cut grass from the lawnmower bag into big paper bags. Carl Sagan was running around in the parts we already cut and lying on his back and rubbing his back in the grass, and I told him, If you keep doing that you're going to turn green, you don't want to take another bath, do you? And then he started crying again because he recognized the word *bath*.

After I helped Ronnie for a while I went inside, and Terra was done vacuuming the living room and she was trying to get out the poop stains from the carpet. I helped her spray the cleaning spray on the stains and Terra scrubbed them with a scrubber but it didn't do much, you could still see the stains there, or even when it did get out the stain it made that part of the carpet look lighter than the carpet around it. Terra said maybe we should have used a carpet cleaner instead of the one we used and I said, But it says *multi-purpose*, is cleaning carpets not one of the multiple purposes? And then I looked on the label and it wasn't.

Steve said maybe we can just cover the stains with rugs, and Terra said that's a great idea, so the guys went to Goodwill to find some rugs that weren't too old and dirty. Meanwhile me and Terra went into my mom's room with garbage bags and we wore gloves that we found in the garage, and it was like we were exploring an alien planet except we didn't have entire space suits, just the gloves. We put all my mom's old coupon flyers in the bags along with some other trash from her closet like shopping bags and empty boxes and crumpled Kleenexes, there were SO many crumpled Kleenexes. When we finished we had fifteen garbage bags full, and I said, Aye yai yai, how can one person make so much garbage!

We took the bags outside and Ronnie was almost done with the lawn by then. He looked kind of funny too, because he took off his T-shirt earlier and now it was sticking out of the back of his shorts like a ponytail. Ronnie saw us with the garbage bags and he said don't leave those on the driveway, put them in the garage for now and we'll take them to the dumpsters later. And then Ronnie used his shirt to wipe off the sweat from his face and I asked him does he want a LOX? and he said sure, so I gave him one of the ones that Steve put in our refrigerator. I told him, Remind me to tell you later about how you can get a free BMW.

The guys got back from Goodwill with some rugs and they got Febreeze also for the wet dog smell, and some potted plants that were Zed's idea. We unrolled the rugs and Terra vacuumed them, and they covered all the poop stains except a couple in the corner of the living room. So Zed just put a plant there. And then we sprayed Febreeze all over, we used SO much Febreeze, and it was supposed to get rid of the smell and it did mostly, but then everything just smelled like Febreeze.

Ronnie came inside and he said, Great job, and I said I'm sure that the social worker is going to be really impressed at how clean and Febreeze-smelling the house is now. He said don't tell her that we cleaned up, just pretend it's like this all the time, and I said I wish I didn't have to pretend. I said, I wish we did this every weekend, because the grass is going to get longer and the house is going to get dirty and smelly and filled with garbage, and we'll have to clean it up all over again. And then Ronnie went back outside because he had more work to do.

After lunch Terra told me to rest for a while, I shouldn't strain myself too much because I'm still recovering from my accident. So I rested with Carl Sagan on the sofa and everyone else got back to work getting the house in order. The guys scrubbed the tub and tiles in the bathroom and Terra swept and mopped the floor of the kitchen so it's not all sticky, and I watched them and I watched Ronnie outside, and I thought maybe if my dad was still alive I'd be watching HIM mow the lawn and clean out the leaves from the gutters, and maybe if my mom wasn't in the behavioral health hospital I'd be watching HER sweep the spiderwebs from the ceilings with a broom.

And then I started wondering, What the heck is a dad anyway? I mean, if you're talking about a biological dad I had one, but what about a non-biological dad? If it's someone to protect you from bad stuff that happens and someone you can help mow the lawn and clean the house, then I have Ronnie and Terra, and if it's someone you can look up to and follow in their footsteps, then I have my hero Dr. Sagan, and if it's someone who you can laugh and drive places with, then the guys did that too, so what's the difference? And why is it that the more I think about that word—*dad*—the less I know what it means? It's the same with words like *love* and *truth* and *bravery* too, the more I think about them and say them over, the less sense they make. Love. Truth. Bravery. Bravery. Truth. Love. It's like, I know those things are out there, I know they exist, but the more I think about them the more it feels like they're all talking about a lot of different things put together, or they're talking about the same thing, but . . . what?

Do you know?

Do you guys have a word for it?

NEW RECORDING 49
15M 9S

The social worker from DHS just left. But so much other stuff happened too, I think my head's going to explode. Except it's not really going to explode, it's just a metaphor. It means I'm overwhelmed. And I want to tell you guys what happened but I don't want to leave anything out, so I'll start from the beginning.

Ronnie said yesterday that it's better if the guys aren't here this morning, that way when the social worker gets here it won't look like there are strange men hanging around the house. I said even if they're a little strange they're still my friends, and Zed laughed and said he agrees with Ronnie. I told Zed if he needs to write down more of his thoughts, then him and Steve can go to the public library, they have computers there too. He said it was a great idea.

So this morning it was just me and Ronnie and Terra

getting ready for the social worker. We got a big pitcher from the cupboard and washed it and filled it with ice water, and we put the pitcher and some glasses on the coffee table. Ronnie said that when the social worker gets here we'll have her sit in the Lay-Z-Boy, and the three of us are going to sit on the sofa because that'll show solidarity. I said that's a great idea because then the social worker will feel comfortable too. Ronnie told me just try to sit still, he's going to do most of the talking, and if the social worker asks me any questions don't answer them unless he gives me the signal.

Ronnie started practicing with us everything he's going to say to the social worker, but then our house phone rang and Ronnie answered it. He said, Hello? and then he said, How did you get this number? and then he said, We're not doing any interviews, and he hung up. I asked Ronnie, Who was that? and he said it was a reporter and then he went to get his laptop, and Terra asked him what did they want? and Ronnie said Lander Civet mentioned me and my Golden iPod in an interview. Ronnie found the interview and showed it to us, and then I logged into my e-mail and I had a ton of new messages and some of them were from reporters who want to interview me!

I said, This is SO cool, I'm famous! and Ronnie said it's pretty cool, yeah, but we can't talk to any reporters right now, not under current circumstances. I asked him why not, isn't that what he helps his clients do, so what's the difference? And he said the difference is that I'm his brother. The phone started ringing again and Ronnie unplugged the line and then there was a knock at the door and Ronnie said, That must be the social worker. But it wasn't the social worker—it was a reporter from Channel 5 Action News!

The news reporter asked Ronnie, Does Alex Petroski live here? and he told her we're not doing any interviews, and she said she just wants a few words with me and then she saw me over Ronnie's shoulder and I waved to her and Ronnie shut the door. She knocked again but Ronnie didn't open it, and I looked through the window and I saw the Channel 5 Mobile Action News Team van parked across the street! It had a tall satellite tower with a curly red cable that curled all the way down to the van, and some joggers ran by and they stopped to look at the van and so did a mom pushing a stroller, and then Ronnie told me to come away from the window. He said, I can't believe this, and there was a knock at the door again and Ronnie went to tell the reporter to go away again, except this time it was the social worker!

The social worker said her name is Juanita. She was holding a black leather folder in one hand and Ronnie shook her other hand and told her to please come in, don't mind all the commotion outside. Juanita came up to me and held out her hand and she said, Hi, you must be Alex, and I looked at Ronnie and he nodded so I shook Juanita's hand and I said it's nice to meet her. Ronnie asked her, Can we get you something to drink, some coffee or water? and she said she just had her morning coffee so water would be great, and I said, I'll pour it! and then I covered my mouth because I forgot to wait for Ronnie's signal.

I went to the coffee table and lifted the water pitcher and it was SO heavy, and Juanita shook hands with Terra and Terra said she's my half sister and I wanted to hug her, except I was holding the pitcher and I didn't want to spill the water.

Juanita sat down in the Lay-Z-Boy but she didn't recline it, and Ronnie and Terra sat down on the sofa and there was a space in between for me, and it was just like we practiced, everything was going according to plan. I gave Juanita the glass and her fingers were wrinkly and her nails had cracked red nail polish, and she said, Thank you, you have a lovely home, and I didn't tell her we cleaned it yesterday.

Juanita took a sip of her water, and Ronnie said that as she can see, I have a safe and stable environment here, and then he started telling her what we practiced, about how my accident and our mom going missing was just a bad coincidence, it was just unfortunate timing, and he's here now and he's going to keep me from getting into any more trouble and it doesn't make sense to remove me from his care. But before he could finish saying everything Juanita put up her hand that wasn't holding the water and she said, Don't worry, I'm not here to break up your family.

I thought, Whew, that's a relief! and I looked at Ronnie, and him and Terra looked at each other and I could tell they were thinking the same thing. But I could tell they were thinking something else too. And then Ronnie looked at Juanita again and he said, That's great, I guess there's not much else to discuss?

Juanita put down her water and she opened her leather folder, and inside the folder was her iPad. She opened some stuff on the iPad and she said she's glad we're all finally meeting in person, and then she started telling us all the things she knows about us. She said she knows that my mom lost her job a few years ago and lost her driver's license too. She said she knows that Ronnie moved to LA after college to be a sports agent and that he was in Detroit recently for work, and that I went to a rocket festival in New Mexico by myself and I have a dog named Carl Sagan after my all-time hero. She said sometimes I go on the roof of my house to see where my mom goes on her walks, and that's what I was doing when

I had my accident and Terra took me to the hospital. Ronnie asked her how does she know all that and she said she's been talking to my teachers and counselor and our neighbors, and my mom's doctors and my doctors and she found Ronnie's profile on his company's website and talked to someone from his work too, and this morning she came across a news article about Lander Civet and a Golden iPod.

And then Ronnie wasn't saying what we practiced anymore. He was telling her the stuff we talked about a couple of days ago, about how I'm going to go live with him in LA for now and then we're going to move our mom there too and sell the house, and if we need to we'll find her a behavioral health hospital there and he'll become my legal guardian and a lot of other stuff that we didn't even talk about! Ronnie said he's here now, isn't he? Isn't that what matters? and I looked at Terra and she looked at me, and Juanita said, Yes, that matters, and again, I'm not here to break apart your family.

Juanita said it's good that Ronnie's thinking about the future, that's what she's here to help us do, she's on our side, but it makes things harder if we leave the state. She asked Ronnie do we have relatives or close family friends in Colorado that I can stay with, and Ronnie said we don't, and Terra said what's the difference between me staying with relatives in Colorado and me staying with

Ronnie in LA, because either way I'm in a different home. And Juanita told us to think about what our mom might want once she's better, once she's out of the hospital.

And Ronnie looked down at the pitcher of water, and I thought that our mom would probably want to go someplace familiar, someplace where she already knows the channel numbers for her favorite shows and where everything is in the cupboards. Someplace she can go for walks but where there's someone to make sure she doesn't walk too far. And someplace where I am and Ronnie is, and where there are pictures of all of us and my dad on the wall in her room. She'd probably want to come home, just like I wanted to come home.

Juanita asked Ronnie is there some way he can keep doing his job from here in Colorado, and Ronnie still didn't say anything, he picked up his phone from the table but not because he got a call or text or anything, just to hold it in his hand. And then Juanita was saying a lot of other stuff but I wasn't paying attention because I was watching Ronnie, and Ronnie kept staring at the water pitcher, and his hand that was holding the phone was turning white.

Then it got really quiet all of a sudden. And I noticed that Juanita had stopped talking, and she was looking at the potted plant in the corner of the room, and Terra was looking at Ronnie, and Ronnie was looking at the water pitcher, and it was almost like we were in space, we were in a vacuum and everything was silent and floating. And the sun was coming through the windows of our living room and there were little pieces of dust floating in the sunbeams, and I thought, isn't it interesting that a couple of weeks ago Ronnie was in LA and I didn't even know I had a Terra, and now the three of us are sitting together on the same sofa for the first time, and we all have the same dad and we're all here because of my dad, he brought us all together, even after he died . . . and I looked at Terra and I looked at Ronnie and I saw the same green eyes, and it felt like our dad was there in the room with us too, not like a ghost or anything, not watching us, but everywhere. He was in Ronnie and Terra's eyes and he was in their faces and their skin and hair, and he was in my face and my skin and hair and these are like his shadows, they're how we know he existed, that he was real, and he used to walk around on the carpet in the living room and drink from the same water glasses and those are shadows also, and his back- and butt-prints were still in the Lay-Z-Boy where Juanita was sitting, that's a shadow too! And if I'm still seeing them, still seeing his shadows, still learning things from Terra and Ronnie and the internet about him that I didn't know before, then, doesn't that mean that even though he died there's something about him that keeps living?

That there's something four-dimensional, a tesseract, that never dies and we can never really see, and what if . . . what if these things I've been trying to figure out, like the meaning of love and bravery and truth, what if the reason they're so hard to see is because they're ALSO tesseracts. What if they're the SAME tesseract? What if the times when we feel love and act brave and tell the truth are all the times we're four-dimensional, the times we're as big and everywhere as the cosmos, the times when we remember, like, REALLY remember, really KNOW, that we're made of starstuff and we're human beings from the planet Earth, human beings with dads that died when we were three and older brothers who live in LA, and moms who have schizophrenia and Terras we didn't know about and heroes who wear turtlenecks and friends with Zen cones and side adventures and sensitive digestive systems and . . . And! These words we try to use to describe it, to describe that feeling, these words like *love* and *bravery* and *truth*, the reason they can't describe it all the way, and the reason that sounds or music or pictures can't describe it all the way either, is because THEY'RE all shadows too! WORDS ARE SHADOWS TOO!

And I guess I said that last part out loud because everyone turned their heads to look at me, and I was standing up, I think because I was thinking about floating. And since I was already up, I started pouring water for Ronnie even though he told me to sit still. I was pouring the water and it was splashing on the sides of the glass and a few drops spilled on the coffee table but I kept pouring, and I could feel everyone watching me but I didn't want to take my eyes off the pitcher because I didn't want to spill any more, and it got easier to pour as the water went from the pitcher to the glass and made the pitcher lighter and then I put down the pitcher and I gave the glass to Ronnie. I knew he wasn't thirsty but I knew he needed the water.

Ronnie looked at me and then he looked at the glass, and then he put down his phone and took the glass from me. And I almost forgot how quiet it was until Juanita started talking again.

Juanita said that I'm really fortunate. She said that even with everything that's happened I'm out of danger now, and I'm interested in school and I've learned to take care of myself, that's a really good sign, that's really lucky, I must have really good role models in my life. Then she closed her iPad folder and folded her hands over it, and she started saying that a lot of kids she sees aren't that lucky, how just yesterday there was . . . and then Juanita stopped talking and I noticed the rings around her eyes, they were just like my mom's eyes, and I wanted to ask what happened yesterday but it didn't feel like the right thing to ask.

And then we all heard crying sounds coming from the bedroom. And Juanita asked, Is that him? and I looked at Ronnie and he nodded, and I asked her does she want to meet Carl Sagan and she said yes, she loves dogs. So I opened my bedroom door and he ran out and sniffed Juanita's hand, and his tail was curled but he let her pet him a little before he ran back behind my legs. I said, I know Carl Sagan's a scaredy cat right now but if I train him to be a guard dog, then can he be my legal guardian? Everyone laughed and Juanita said, Unfortunately not, and I told her I know, I was just making a joke.

Juanita said she has to go to another appointment but let's meet again next week, and she gave Ronnie her card and she gave me her card too, and she said thank you for the water and wished me good luck with my Golden iPod.

The Channel 5 Mobile Action News Team van wasn't outside anymore by the time Juanita left. Ronnie closed the front door and the four of us stood by it, and we were all quiet for a while. And then Terra said we don't have to do what Juanita told us, we could stall for time and I could still go with Ronnie to LA, and maybe it'll turn out that my mom gets better more quickly and can come back to the house to take care of me, that way he won't miss work.

Then Ronnie looked at me and he said No, Juanita's

right, even if our mom comes out of the hospital it'd still be better if he was around. And I said, Are you saying what I think you're saying? and Ronnie nodded, and then Terra said but what about his job? and Ronnie said he'll try to work it out with his agency, maybe he can do something from Colorado that doesn't involve as much traveling, or if not he'll find a different job.

And we all stood there for a while and looked at each other, and then Terra's nose started twitching and Ronnie scrunched up his face, and then I smelled it too and we all looked at Carl Sagan and I said, OH JUST GREAT, and I went to get the Febreeze.

NEW RECORDING 50
3M 7S

Hi guys. Sorry I haven't recorded anything in a while. I've been SO busy. I got my staples and stitches out at the hospital and it's still pink around my scars and there's still little dots where the staples were, but Dr. Clemens said I'm healing nicely. There are no signs of permanent damage. I said, Does that mean I get a clean bill of health? and she said it does, and then I took out my wallet and waited for her to give me one but she never did.

I was also busy because there were more articles that came out about my Golden iPod, and Lander tweeted about it too and now the donation page is at 281 percent! And it's still going. Benji e-mailed me and told me he saw Lander's tweets on CNN and he thought it was so cool, and I got e-mails from some other kids at school also and I had no idea they were interested in space or rockets or anything, which is good news, maybe now I can get them to join the Rockview Planetary Society. I posted on Rocketforum to thank everyone for donating and I uploaded some pictures of how my scars are healing too, and Ken Russell said that's going to be a great story when I'm older. I said it's a pretty great story right now.

A lot of people on Rocketforum were asking me what am I going to do with the outstanding money. I told Ronnie we should use it for our mom's hospital bills, and Steve said we should take advantage of all this attention we're getting and do a bunch of interviews and that way we'll raise even more money. But Ronnie said no, no interviews, he doesn't want any more of our family's private matters out in public. He said also let him worry about our mom's bills, any extra money we raise is going into a fund to pay for my college.

Tonight we all went to Johnny Rockets for dinner finally to celebrate, just like Ronnie promised. The closest one to us is forty minutes away, and I got a cheeseburger and fries and apple pie à la mode and it was so good. Afterwards we waited for a call from my mom and then she called. She's allowed to talk on the phone now but only for ten minutes a day, and she talked with Ronnie for four minutes and then she talked with me for six minutes. I asked her, How are you feeling and do you still think I'm an alien? and she said that she's feeling better than before and she knows I'm her Alex. I told her about the Golden iPod and how Lander Civet invited us to the Mars launch and his assistant is e-mailing us the tickets, and I asked my mom can she come? And she said she's so proud of me but she can't leave right now. I asked her, When can we come visit again because I still have to bring you some things for your room, and she said she needs some more time because she wants to be good for me. I told her, I love you even when you're not good, and she said she loves me too. She said they have the NASA channel at the behavioral health hospital and one of the techs is going to put it on for the Mars launch so that way she can watch it, and then she had to go because her ten minutes were over.

NEW RECORDING 51
2M 43S

I'm on a plane! I've been on a bike and a skateboard and a scooter and in a car and canoe and on a train, and now I've been on an airplane, so I just need to ride a helicopter and a motorcycle and a unicycle and a hot-air balloon and a Segway and Jet Ski and dune buggy and of course a space capsule and space rover, and then I would've tried every form of human transpor—oh! Snow-mobiles too. I forgot about snowmobiles.

Terra let me have her seat by the window even though my ticket was for the seat in the middle. I asked Terra, Why aren't the seats lined up with the windows? and she said she has no idea. I was looking out the window when our plane took off and the cars got really small until they looked like ants and then like grains of sand, and then I couldn't even see them and that's when I knew we were definitely in the stratosphere—the part of the atmosphere, not the building in Las Vegas.

Steve and Zed couldn't come with us because Lander's assistant only got plane tickets and a hotel for me and Ronnie and Terra and Carl Sagan, except he doesn't need a plane ticket because he's a dog. When we were saying good-bye, Zed gave me a thick stack of printouts and I said, What's this? and he said it's the first part of the new book he's writing—that's what he's been working on this whole time. He said he's dedicating the book to me and he wants me to read it and let him know what I think. The book is called *Journey to the Unseen Star: Rediscovering Childhood in an Accelerating Age.* I told him it's a good title but he can probably come up with something shorter.

Steve gave me a really big hug before they left, a good hug, not like the hugs before where he only used his arms. I asked him, Are you still sad about Terra? and he said sometimes he is but he'll be OK. He said he's going to read Zed's book too and he really wants to talk about it with me when he's done. He said we could keep the cans of LOX he put in our fridge also, and then he gave me one of the cellphones he got from doing his personal business. I said, Aren't you going to sell this on eBay? and Steve said he wants me to have it, he even put in a prepay card so that way we can stay in touch, and maybe we can all hang out if I'm ever in LA.

I tried reading Zed's book after our plane took off but I couldn't concentrate. I was too excited. I looked out the window again and we were even higher, and I couldn't tell where the roads and buildings were anymore and it was just like my hero said, that from a certain height you can't even tell there's intelligent life on our own planet.

So if you guys come to Earth, make sure you look closely enough.

NEW RECORDING 52
6M 9S

Hi guys, this is the last recording I'm making on the Golden iPod. But don't worry! I can take pictures and record video on the phone Steve gave me so I'm going to start doing that instead. It's perfect because the phone's already gold.

After our plane landed in Florida we got our rental car and dropped off our bags at the hotel, and then we drove to Cape Canaveral. When we got there CivSpaceScott was there to meet us, and he had on his gray CivSpace polo shirt just like at SHARF. Scott took us to the launch site and we saw the Cloud 9 rocket with the Mars satellite up close through a chain link fence and it was SO cool. He took us to NASA's command center too, except it didn't have big glass windows like in *Contact*, it just had a huge screen with a live stream of the launch site and a bunch of charts and graphs. Nathan would probably love that screen because he could write so much tiny computer code on it.

Lander Civet isn't here yet, he's not coming until tomorrow, but I met a bunch of other people from CivSpace and they said they heard about me, and they asked to see my Golden iPod. I met some scientists from NASA also, and I met Dr. Judith Bloomington and . . . um . . .

Anyway . . . We watched them test-fire the rocket thrusters, and then we said see you tomorrow to Scott and we had dinner at a restaurant near our hotel. Ronnie told me that his prospective client in Detroit heard about my Golden iPod and he's a big fan of CivSpace too, he even wants to live on Mars one day. I told Ronnie, That's great news, does that mean that he wants you to be his agent and what if you leave with that client and your other ones and start your own sports agency like in that one movie starring Tom Cruise?

Ronnie laughed and said unfortunately real life doesn't always work like that. He said the kid's mom and dad have to do what's best for their family, and so does he, that's why he referred them to one of his co-workers. Terra said that's too bad, and Ronnie said it is what it is, and I finished my fish and chips and Terra said how about let's go for a walk and get ice cream along the way, she has something she wants to talk to me about. So we got the check and Ronnie went back to our room to make some phone calls, and

Terra and me took Carl Sagan for a walk on the beach.

This was the first time Carl Sagan has ever seen the ocean up close. He kept crying at the water at first, he didn't like it probably because it reminded him of taking a bath. But then after a while he didn't really care. The sky was getting dark and there were some people out but not as many as Venice Beach, and the water was warm and darker than the sky. The three of us stood in the shallow part and we let the waves come over our feet, and we ate our ice cream and listened to the peacefulness.

Then I asked Terra, What are you thinking about? and she said, A lot of things. I said, Can you tell me some of those things? and she hugged me to her side and crumpled up the ice cream wrapper, and she put it in her pocket. I crumpled up my wrapper too and put it in my own pocket, and I told Terra, Ronnie said that being an adult means taking responsibility for your actions, so I'm glad we're both doing that. Terra laughed and she said that sometimes it means taking responsibility even for the things you're not responsible for, and also, don't worry about being an adult just yet. She said that I have a good brother, and I said I have a good Terra too, and she said I can tell people she's my half sister as much as I want, she's totally proud to be my half sister.

I asked Terra what's going to happen after this? What's going to happen after the launch? Is she going to come live in Rockview with me and Ronnie and my mom when my mom gets out of her behavioral health hospital? Terra said that I'm a sweetheart but she can't stay with us, and I said, Why not? I told her we have restaurants in Rockview too so she can have her same job, and I know she doesn't have friends here but I'll be her friend, and every day when I'm back from my school and Ronnie's back from his work and she's back from her restaurant we can all make dinner and watch *Contact* together and look at the stars but not from any roofs, I've learned my lesson.

Terra hugged me and told me she's sorry, she knows she swore we'd stick together. Terra said she's definitely going to come visit but that I inspired her. She said that like how there's rockets and astronomy for me, there's something for her, she just doesn't know what it is yet. She said she wants to figure that out, but first she wants to go back home and spend some time with her mom and Howard. She asked me do I understand why, and I said I do, life is four-dimensional, and Terra laughed again.

We threw away our ice cream wrappers and walked back to the hotel, and by then the sky was completely dark and the wind was warm but nice, and when we got back to our room Ronnie was on his laptop again. I asked him, How did your calls go? and he said they went great, he talked to some of his old coaches from college and he's going to meet a few of their players when we get back to Colorado. Then Ronnie got up to make some coffee and Terra went to take a shower, and I came out on the balcony with Carl Sagan.

I tried to see the launch site from here but I couldn't, so I went to the live stream on my new phone and I held it up to where the site would be if there weren't any houses blocking the way. The rocket was lit up on the screen and standing straight and tall by itself, and I thought about how one day there's going to be another big rocket, one that I made with help from a lot of my friends, and this Golden iPod is going to be on it.

And it's going to launch into the sky and leave our stratosphere and go past our moon and Mars and the asteroid belt and outer planets and Pluto and into deep space, and maybe you're going to find it.

And I wonder what'll happen when you DO find it. I wonder what you're going to think when you listen to these recordings, when you hear the sounds of a boy from planet Earth trying to be brave and a boy trying to find the truth, and a boy who loves his family and friends and his dog that he named after his hero.

Because I realized what Zed meant when he said, You already have it. And I agree.

« END OF RECORDINGS »

ACKNOWLEDGMENTS

This novel has very much been a rocket of its own—launch could not have been possible without the help of a good number of friends. Deepest thanks to all my fellow wanderers, including: Jessica Craig, for her unwavering support and belief in me. Jess Dandino Garrison and Anthea Townsend, for guiding me through unfamiliar territory, and for helping peel open the layers to find what the book was really about. John Hering, for generosity, friendship, and a space to write by the beach in California. Maria Cardona, Marina Penalva, Leticia Vila-Sanjuán, Anna Soler-Pont, and the rest of the Pontas team, for helping seed this story around the globe. Drake Baer and Ian Alas, for advice on early drafts and in life. Bethany Sumner, for stories from a different time and place. Jess Frisina, Pamela Safronoff, and Sarah Sallen, for insights into social work and Child Protective Services. Gratitude also to Courtney Balestier, Amanda Natividad, Mikaela Akerman, Robin Sloan, Dan Safronoff, Jason Roos, Andrew Horng, and the truly stellar teams at Penguin Young Readers (on both sides of the Atlantic!).

Last but never least, thank you to Kickstarter, and to all the backers of my previous novel, *These Days*. I would not be here without you.